TOWER of EVIL

TOWER of EVIL

Mary Main

WESTWIND®
Troll Associates

For my mother,
who believed

"I am so framed by God
(his grace be blest)
that me your misery touches not,
nor me doth yonder
burning with its flame molest."

Canto 2, *Dante's Inferno*

The human heart has hidden treasures,
In secret kept, in silence sealed.

Charlotte Brontë

CHAPTER

ONE

Fog gives me the creeps. I'm not talking about the cool mist that burns off the ocean on summer mornings. That's romantic, poetic even. I mean the heavy gray stuff that seeps through your pores into your skin until you can't stop shivering. That's the kind of fog that wrapped itself around me as I hiked over the dunes on my first day in California.

I closed my eyes and breathed the fishy air. The dull thud of waves filled my head. I could almost believe I was back home on Cape Cod, and everything was the way it used to be. Before the fire. Before Mom and Dad died. I opened my eyes to stop the remembering, and

7

the rough coastline of Rock Cove brought me back to reality. Face it, Tory, I told myself. Your old life is gone forever.

I turned and walked along the shore, knowing I'd never get used to living with Aunt Julia in this damp, depressing place. I hardly knew her and wondered if I were as welcome as she'd claimed on our ride from the airport. I felt cold inside, as if the fog had worked its way through my sweater and skin into my bones, and I walked faster.

On my left, boulders swept up from the water to form a steep cliff. I stopped and stared. A round black structure loomed on top. Only a weird building, I told myself. But I studied it in disbelief. How could this place be here? Now? It looked thousands of years old, like the temples I'd seen in one of Dad's books. Horrible pictures streamed into my mind: animal bones on altars, little kids thrown into fires, priests slashing their faces to appease angry gods. Ancient religions could be very unforgiving. And gruesome.

As I stared, unconsciously my fingers sought the gold charm at my throat. What was this place? No windows opened on the bottom of the building, just black rocks overlapping like a giant puzzle. On the second story, a ring of balconies with red glass doors hugged the rock. Above it all, a domed roof smoldered with red light. Smoke gushed into the fog from a crag of chimney that cleft the dome.

"Aunt Julia never told me about this," I whispered, and the sound of my own voice made me jump. The smell of smoke stung the air. Someone was using the place right now. What were they were doing inside those jagged black walls?

"Tory Madison?"

I gasped at the deep voice behind me and spun around.

A boy wrapped in a red beach towel smiled at me. "Didn't mean to scare you." He held out his hand. "I'm Greg Howatt."

He was a typical guy. Brown eyes, brown hair and freckles. What had I expected? A crazed demon? I guessed he was a couple of years older than I am, sixteen maybe. I shook his hand. "You shouldn't sneak up on people like that."

He grinned. "Sorry."

"That's okay." My heart still raced in my chest. "Was that you I saw surfing earlier?"

"Yeah. Too bad the waves are lousy." He coiled the towel around his neck. His chest and arms looked as strong as my gymnastics coach.

I pointed a toe into the sand and stretched my leg. Stiff muscles. I hadn't worked out in weeks. "How do you know my name?" I asked.

"You're Julia's niece, aren't you? She said you were coming today."

"You know my aunt?"

"Oh, sure. Everybody knows Julia. She's the most famous architect in L.A."

I glanced up at the black building. "She didn't design this monstrosity, did she?"

Greg laughed. "No."

"What is it, anyway?"

"That's Dag's house."

"Somebody *lives* there?"

"Believe it or not. Ever hear of the rock group Cyclone? Dag Ashton plays lead guitar."

"Cyclone? Sure." I'd seen the band on TV once but only remembered the singer, Kelsey Woodruff, short and blond. I couldn't think what Dag Ashton looked like. Black cape and fangs dripping blood? If he matched his house, the answer was yes.

Greg watched a flock of seagulls disappear into the fog. He had a straight nose, and a square jaw that made him look kind of stubborn. But his brown eyes were soft as the velvet Mom used in her quilts. "Julia told me about your parents," he said. "That's really tough."

"Yeah."

He was quiet, as if he didn't know what more to say. I stared down at the sand. I couldn't talk about Mom and Dad. Ever since they died, I felt raw inside. Just thinking about them made me sadder than I ever thought I could be.

"Are you shell hunting?" he asked, noticing the chipped sand dollar in my hand.

I nodded.

"Any luck?" His smile was friendly.

"Not yet." I tossed the broken sand dollar away.

"Don't worry. You'll spot some. My girlfriend has a great shell collection. All from around here."

11

"Who's your girlfriend?" I asked.

"Well, ex-girlfriend. Delia . . . Delia Krieger. She's been up north at her mother's for a couple of weeks. It's been pretty quiet around here." He still liked her, I could tell.

"Oh." I patted my hair, suddenly aware that my new jeans were stiff and geeky-looking; likewise for my bulky wool cardigan. My red hair always frizzed up in the fog, and my freckles weren't delicately sprinkled like Greg's but plastered all over my face.

"That's a cool necklace." Greg stared at my throat. "What's the charm on it?"

"A sword."

He grinned. "To fight off the bad guys?"

"You could say that." I reached up and pressed the tip of the little sword, liking the sharp sting on my fingertip. "Mom and Dad gave it to me on my birthday. They said . . . Well, they said a lot of things."

"Want to tell me, or am I butting in?"

"That's funny. My friends tell me I'm the one who's too nosy." I swirled a toe through the sand. "It's not that I don't want to tell you, but . . . I can't always remember. When they died, you know . . . it was a shock."

"Yeah." His voice was soft.

"One thing my dad told me is that there's a whole world out there we can't see. He taught theology at the university, so he knew all about history and religions and stuff."

"You mean, like aliens?"

"No. More like good and evil. Those two are always warring. He said the sword is my weapon."

Greg lifted an eyebrow. "So, it's to fight the invisible bad guys?"

"Something like that. I didn't always understand my dad's theories. But . . . they had this made for me. It's one of a kind. I always wear it." I didn't tell him that it made me feel safe. And it was all I had left of Mom and Dad.

I looked up at the house on the cliff. "Does Dag Ashton live alone?"

"Nope. His daughter, Elissa, lives there too. She's twelve." He was quiet for awhile, and when he spoke his voice was low. "Her mom killed herself last summer."

"You mean suicide?" I felt cold all over.

He nodded.

"How?"

"She jumped off Elissa's balcony. Landed right there." He pointed to a huge pile of rocks in the ocean. "Dag found her."

"That's awful! Are you sure it wasn't an accident?"

"It could have been, but nobody thinks so." He folded his arms. "Donna Jean was really depressed. Hardly ever came out of the house. Once, she hitchhiked into Malibu in her robe and nightgown with Elissa. Burst into the Sunset Cafe and started screaming about getting away. Something about blood all over the house. The police checked it out but couldn't find anything. Everyone thought she'd lost it."

"What do you think?"

He shrugged. "Dag tried to get her to a shrink, but she wouldn't go for it. There's one thing about her death they never figured out."

"What?"

"The palms of her hands had blisters on them, like she'd grabbed hot coals or something."

I rubbed my palms on my jeans. "Weird."

14

"Yeah. Dag was really broken up over the whole thing. I was building shelves in his house at the time. He didn't pick up his guitar for days after it happened."

"You worked in there?"

He nodded. "I like to build things. But don't blame me for the way the place looks. Dag has wild ideas. Your aunt calls it organic architecture. That's when a building looks like it grew from the ground through an act of nature."

I glanced up at the black house. "Nature must have gone berserk that day."

Greg's grin made me feel better. "It's not bad once you get used to it."

"I don't think I'll ever get used to it." Just knowing it hovered above us on the cliff made me feel a little scared. But I wanted to see the inside too. Weird stuff made me wary. Also curious.

Greg shivered. "I'm freezing. Want to walk back with me?"

I glanced up the beach at Aunt Julia's house. The glass front shimmered in the fog. A balcony stuck out from my room on the second story—the gigantic gray room I'd hated on

15

sight. My aunt had gotten some kind of award for designing the house, but I didn't think it was that great. It reminded me of a packing crate with windows. "Think I'll see if I can find a checkered periwinkle. We don't have them on the Cape."

"Good luck." Greg pulled his towel tight around his shoulders. "I have a job in L. A. this week, so I'm staying in the city at my brother's. But I'll be at your aunt's party on the Fourth. Delia should be back home by then." He glanced up at the house. "Dag and Elissa are invited, too, but who knows if they'll show up . . . . See you next Sunday, okay?"

"Sure." I smiled. "Nice meeting you."

"Same here." He hoisted his surfboard under his arm and hiked off over the dunes. Greg was a lot more talkative than the guys I knew back home. Maybe my aunt's party wouldn't be as boring as I'd thought. I watched him open the gate of the homey, old-fashioned-looking blue and white colonial house near Aunt Julia's angular modern one. He disappeared inside, and the beach seemed lonely again.

Waves crashed behind me, and somewhere in the fog seagulls shrieked, fighting over food. I found my eyes drawn to the black tower again. A sudden movement on the balcony made me draw in my breath. A pale and pretty girl stood there, her dark hair swinging over her long white dress. She looked right at me, then backed out of sight. For a second, I even thought I'd imagined her. But no, I could see her white dress fluttering slightly out of the doorway.

"Elissa?" I called.

My only answer was the clatter of the doors on the balcony slamming shut.

CHAPTER

TWO

I didn't spend much time at the beach that first week in California, but I thought a lot about the girl on the balcony. For some reason she fascinated me. The more I thought about her, the more I wanted to see her again. The few times I made it to the beach, I walked to the black house, and stood there, looking up at the strange tomb-like building. But no one ever appeared again.

Aunt Julia insisted on giving me the super-deluxe sightseeing tour: Universal Studios, Disneyland, Knott's Berry Farm. I had to give her credit. If life had been normal, I would have had a great time.

Life wasn't normal, though. I'd escaped a harrowing fire, but at a terrible cost. I'd lost my parents, my anchor. Through it all I grieved inwardly.

The weather, as if to try and burn my unhappiness right out of me, was hot and sunny. Then it seemed to take the hint, and we had a few days of gray drizzle. It didn't matter. I felt lonely when it was bright, and lonely when it was dank. I'd lost my parents, and it seemed the ache would never disappear.

The sun finally came out on Sunday, July Fourth, right before I climbed the stairs to shower and dress for the party. My freckles had gone wild from all the sun of the past week, and my red hair ballooned around my face, thanks to the near-constant sea spray and fog. I swished blusher over my cheeks, rubbed on lip gloss, and pulled my hair into the high ponytail I wore in gymnastics meets. I thought of the time I'd competed in the state finals. My stomach had gone into spasms as I waited for my turn. I felt almost that tense right now. But once I got out on the floor and started my routine, I forgot to be nervous. Performing always lifted me out of myself into a world of action. We'd come in second, and that wasn't bad.

I straightened my cotton sweater over my shorts and headed downstairs. I hoped Elissa and her father would show up. My aunt had explained that there were only two other families at the cove besides the Ashtons—the Howatts and the Kriegers—so it would be a small party, and that was fine with me.

At the bottom of the stairs, Aunt Julia rushed up to me. She looked so much like Dad that it just about killed me every time I saw her. She had hazel eyes like his, and even shared his habit of pushing up her glasses on her nose. Her light-brown hair was cut straight to her chin, and she was tall and skinny.

Aunt Julia put an arm around my shoulders and led me into the living room between white overstuffed couches and chrome and glass tables. She squeezed my shoulders. "What a lovely sweater, darling. That aqua matches your eyes exactly. You have your mother's eyes, you know. . ."

"Thanks, Aunt Julia."

She stared at me. "In fact, you're the image

of Anne, petite, lovely . . ." Her eyes filled with tears, and she turned away. "Come, Tory, I want you to meet Dr. Krieger."

A stocky man in a blue shirt and bow-tie walked up to us. "Hello, Tory. I'm Stan Krieger. From the big yellow house up the beach." Dr. Krieger's eyes were a strange color, amber with gold flecks in them. Dark brown curls stuck up all over his head.

"Hello," I said.

He smiled and shook my hand. "I'm happy to meet you. I would have visited earlier, but I've been at a medical convention in New York, and Delia's been staying with her mother. Julia told me about your parents. I'm so sorry."

I nodded and bit my lip. Every time somebody said they were sorry, it brought back memories of that awful night. Smoke, flames, the shouts of the firemen. But I knew the doctor was only being polite.

"My Delia's out on the patio," he said. "She's a little older than you, fifteen, but I hope you'll get to know each other." He looked out the window. "Delia needs friends . . ." He let the sentence trail off.

"Darling Stan." My aunt took his arm. "We'd better start the *fajitas* and let Tory get acquainted with the young people."

"Of course, Julia." He smiled at me. "Time to don my chef's apron. Let's chat more later, shall we?"

"Sure, Dr. Krieger."

Out on the patio, Greg stood near the picnic table, talking to a blond girl in flowered leggings and a lime-green top. He looked casual and suntanned in jeans and a sweater. He waved at me, and I strolled over. "Hi, Tory. This is Delia."

Her eyes were the same amber color as her father's, but eyeliner and mascara made them look wide and cat-like. Her short blond hair lifted in a wave over her forehead. Earrings shaped like leaves dangled to her shoulders.

I touched my ponytail, which suddenly seemed childish and dull. Why hadn't I worn my hair in a more sophisticated style, a French twist or something? "Hi," I said lamely.

"Oh, hi." Delia looked me up and down, then glanced out at the beach as if hoping someone would come along and rescue her from the boredom of meeting me.

Greg didn't seem to notice. "How's the shell hunting going, Tory?"

"Great. I found a checkered periwinkle. And a red abalone, too." I turned to Delia. "I hear you have a good collection."

"What?" She fiddled with an earring. "You mean shells? I tossed those stinky things ages ago."

"They don't stink if you boil them," I told her.

"Right." She gave me a long stare. "My dad said you're a big gymnastics champ or something."

"Not really, but I'm into it."

"Planning to try out for the team at school?"

I hadn't thought that far ahead but made an instant decision. "Sure."

A smile arched her lips. "Our team is the best. We won state finals last year. You probably won't make it."

"Are you on the team?"

She looked at me as if I were crazy. "I'm five-nine. Everyone knows only shrimps like you have half a chance at gymnastics."

"Our team wasn't bad either," I told her evenly. "We took second in Massachusetts."

"Good for you." Delia rested her hand possessively on Greg's arm. "How's the surf been lately?"

"Lousy. But then you can ride anything, Dee." He gazed down at her, and his eyes turned soft as melted chocolate.

I wondered what it felt like to have a guy look at you like you were the most gorgeous person on the planet. Pretty good, probably. It didn't seem to make Delia's day, though. She shrugged and stared out at the beach.

My aunt and Dr. Krieger came through the door with platters of food. "Tory, darling, may I bring you a jacket? It's gotten a bit chilly out."

"No, Aunt Julia. I'm okay."

Delia gave me a look, and I wanted to hide under the picnic table. Why did Aunt Julia have to treat me like I was two? My parents had died, but that didn't make me helpless.

I headed for the snacks and grabbed a chip with melted cheese on top. Waves crashed beyond the road, sending a fine spray into the air, and the usual salt tang blended with the spicy scent of peppers and cheese. I'd just reached for another chip when I heard the gate open.

"Elissa! Dag!" Aunt Julia swept across the patio. "How lovely to see you."

I swallowed quickly and stared. Dag Ashton towered over my aunt in his purple T-shirt, leather vest and faded jeans. Thick, black hair billowed around his face and over his shoulders. His silver-blue eyes shone like the ocean on a sunny day. Now, I remembered him from TV. He was a lot better looking in person.

"Dag!" Delia rushed over to him. "I'll take your guitar into the house."

Aunt Julia waved an arm in my direction. "Tory, darling, I'd like you to meet the Ashtons."

I walked over. "Hi Elissa," I said. "I saw you on your balcony one day."

She glanced quickly at her father then back to me. She didn't say anything, just studied me with her gray eyes.

I stared back at her, taking slow breaths, remembering an old daydream. When I was little, I imagined I had a sister. We'd do everything together. Collect shells, build sand castles, ride the waves. In my fantasy, she was smaller than I was, with huge eyes and long black hair. The only thing I hadn't thought of was her name. Elissa. A really beautiful name. Like the sound the waves make when they brush the sand at low tide.

Dag put his arm around Elissa's shoulders, turning her toward a nearby bench. Her white blouse floated around her as she sat and took a sketch book from her shoulder bag.

She's mysterious, I thought, like those paintings of Renaissance angels in history books. I wouldn't have been surprised to see wings sprouting from her back.

"Elissa is never without her sketchbook." Aunt Julia smiled down at me. "She has such talent. She painted the oil over my fireplace, you know. I wish Dag would allow her to have formal training."

I looked quickly at my aunt and then toward the fireplace. "That painting's fantastic," I said honestly. But a cord of tension pulled tight inside me as I gazed at the huge frame. It was an eerie painting of the point. That was what everyone called the rock cliff where Elissa's house sat. How awful. She must have finished the canvas before her mother killed herself—on the very spot Elissa had painted.

Aunt Julia patted my arm. "The child is a prodigy, but I wish she were happier."

I remembered the bitter-cold spray on the jagged rocks and stared at Elissa's thin shoulders. She must miss her mother a lot. Like I missed Mom.

Dag strolled over, greeted my aunt and smiled down at me. He's gorgeous, I thought, even that scar on his left cheek. Long and thin, it made him look exotic and sort of old-worldly, like one of King Arthur's knights. All he needed was a tall steed and a suit of shining armor. He was so tall I had to tip my head back to look at his face.

"Vacationing here, Tory?" His deep, rough voice sounded more like hard rock than the lilting music of Cyclone.

"Well, not exactly." In a way, it was a relief that Dag didn't seem to have heard why I'd ended up here. I didn't have to deal with the pity—or the misguided sympathy of people who couldn't possibly understand my devastation.

He tossed his head, and his black hair swirled around his shoulders. "Rock Cove is an extraordinary place. Full of beauty and wisdom. Especially potent for songwriters and artists."

I tucked a strand of hair into my ponytail. "I like your music. I saw you on TV one time."

"I'm glad." He smiled, and his teeth were white and perfect.

My aunt shoved her glasses up on her nose. "Thanks to Dag, Rock Cove will stay unspoiled. He's the chairman of our environmental association, dear."

"Oh. That's nice."

"Our coast is precious to me." He raked a hand through his shining hair. A large silver ring curved around his index finger. A carved bull's head.

A trickle of cold ran down my spine. Where had I seen a ring like that before?

"Are you staying with us long, Tory?"

My aunt slipped an arm around me. "Tory lost her parents recently, Dag. My brother, Bill, and his dear Anne . . . She'll be living with me from now on."

"I see." His silver-blue eyes pierced into

mine. "Fortunately, death is only a bend in the journey to another life. I'll sing to you tonight, Tory. My music will heal you with the message of renewal."

What was he talking about? How dare he say this to me? Suddenly, adrenalin pumped through my veins like I was about to go on in a meet. "You don't have to do that."

"Oh, but I want to." He looked down at the ring on his finger, then back to me. "In fact, I am compelled to sing to you tonight." He stared at me, and his pupils held tiny pinpoints of flame, reflected from the setting sun. "Destiny has set aside a few moments in time especially for you and me."

"How very thoughtful of you, Dag." My aunt looked impressed.

I should have been impressed, too. But I felt my hand shake as I reached up to brush back my bangs. Would he make a big deal of it and want me to dance with him or something? Would he want to hold my hand in those long, bony fingers? Looking at him, my stomach tightened. Suddenly, I wished I'd never come here.

CHAPTER

THREE

A moment later I wondered why I'd felt so upset. Don't be a geek, I told myself. I could write Amy and Taylor and tell them all about it, and they'd die with jealousy. A big star like Dag singing to *me*.

"I put your guitar in the house, Dag." Delia walked up, glaring at me.

He smiled down at her, and her frown melted into a goo-goo, gaa-gaa look. Gee, I hoped I never acted that obvious. Anyway, Dag wasn't *that* awesome. Or was he? My heartbeat rocketed thinking about what he'd said about destiny. A few moments just for me, later on tonight.

"Thanks, sweetheart." He flung his hair over a shoulder and turned to my aunt, completely ignoring Delia's adoring look. "Julia, I've been thinking. A benefit concert could bring in the funds we need to publicize the building moratorium along the coast. I can't rest until every last developer is out of here. I know you feel the same."

"Why, Dag, what a wonderful idea. And how generous of you."

Delia moved next to him and shoved her arm through his. Aunt Julia glanced at her, and I couldn't tell how she felt about Delia's crush on Dag. I wondered what her father thought. My parents would have hated me hanging all over a guy like that. And let's face it, Dag was old, too.

I listened to the talk about buildings and land deals for a minute, then slipped across the patio to the table where I stared at the Mexican buffet spread out on the red, white, and blue cloth. I slapped a tortilla on a plate and piled it with chicken strips and peppers.

Elissa sat near the fence with her sketch pad, whisking her pencil over the paper. I strolled around the edge of the patio and stopped behind her, looking over her shoulder. What I saw almost made me drop my plate. Me! There on the paper. She'd drawn my sword charm, too, but made it life size. In the drawing, I lunged forward, the sword in my hand. My ponytail flew out behind me. My lips were drawn back over my teeth, and the muscles in my arm bulged. The look in my eyes said I was ready to commit murder.

"God," I said out loud.

Elissa looked up at me, her eyes wide with surprise. "Sorry," I said. "I didn't mean to sneak up on you, but I, uh . . . Your picture kind of shocked me. Why . . . ?"

But before I could ask, Greg's mother stepped up and introduced herself. She was really nice, but she talked on and on, first about Rock Cove and then about what a wonderful person Aunt Julia was. My eyes darted to Elissa's sketch pad. She'd flipped the page and was sketching the ocean.

I felt someone staring at me.

Across the patio, Dag gave me a long, lazy smile as if we shared a secret. His tongue slid slowly along his lower lip. Heat burst in my cheeks, and I turned away. What was Mrs. Howatt saying? I couldn't concentrate. My pulse hammered in my ears as she moved away. Was I having star fever or what? I'd always thought it was dumb the way my friends acted over rock singers. Now, I could hardly eat, I was so shook up. I thought a crush would feel happier than this. Instead, I felt like a motor was revving inside my stomach.

As the sky grew dark, Greg and Dr. Krieger arranged benches around the firepit.

"Are you ready to sing for us, Dag, darling?" My aunt spread cushions on the redwood seats.

"Of course, Julia." He lounged on a bench looking over the fire, and Delia brought his guitar, moving in so close she was practically hugging his side.

I found a place across the fire from them.

Greg eased in next to me. He smelled fresh and clean, like shampoo. "How's it going, kid?"

"Good." After seeing the way he looked at Delia, I knew I didn't stand a chance to be his girlfriend, but I wasn't planning on that, anyway.

On a nearby bench, Elissa stared into the fire, hugging her arms to her sides. I made up my mind to talk to her as soon as Dag finished singing. *I'll find out why she drew that picture*, I thought. I reached up and pressed my sword charm between my fingertips.

Dag tuned his guitar. The fire spit and crackled, blending with the rhythmic sounds of waves and vibrating strings. A muffled boom came from a faraway fireworks show. Stars appeared like lights being switched on in the heavens. Other Fourths of July came to mind: our team marching in the parade down Main Street, clambakes on the beach, Mom's chocolate cake with the flag made out of candy sprinkles. I let myself drift away to the town where I grew up.

Greg nudged me. "What're you thinking about?"

I looked into his brown eyes. "Just . . . things."

Across from us, Dag held his hands over the fire. His long white fingers moved into the flames, and the big ring glowed. His hands throbbed with orange light. I sucked in my breath. Were his fingers on fire? I craned my neck to see better. Only a trick of the light. Still, I breathed faster. He shook his hands, rubbed them together, then picked up his guitar and slapped his fingers against the strings. Thundering sounds filled the patio.

Greg moved closer to me. "Get ready for some hot music."

"I'm ready."

Dag's smile moved over all of us, drawing us to him, binding us together. "Music, like fire, is my power source, neighbors. Tonight, I have a message for you. A message of life that will enflame your hearts and turn them toward truth." His fingers beat against the strings, and the night filled up with the pulsing sounds of the guitar. He launched into *Tennessee Morning*.

I'd heard Kelsey Woodruff sing this song, but Dag's version was better. His rough voice complemented the driving beat, and the music built up inside me until I swayed back and forth, slapping my hands together. Greg let out a whoop. I glanced at Elissa. Still as a stone, she stared into the fire, her hair a shimmering black curtain hiding her face. How could she not respond to that incredible beat?

Dag growled the final chorus, and the song crashed to a close. He paused, then slammed the strings again in a blistering run. "Remember this date, neighbors. Wednesday, July 14th. Ten days from today. Cyclone leaves on tour. Millions around the world will hear our music and be enlightened. A chunk of my profits will go to our ocean cleanup project, as always. Dag Ashton cares about the coast."

Furious clapping broke out, and Greg let out an ear-splitting whistle.

"Will Elissa accompany you?" Dr. Krieger called.

"Lissy's grandparents in Tennessee will keep her while I tour."

I felt a stab of disappointment. Elissa would be leaving in ten days. I wondered how long she'd be gone. She stared into the fire. Was she shivering? I couldn't tell. It might have been the shadows flickering over her shoulders in the firelight.

"Here's to a platinum record." Greg raised his fist in the air.

Dag's lip curled in a smile. "I love you, neighbors. You give me solitude. A beautiful gift. Without the isolation that Rock Cove provides, I couldn't create the words and music that must touch a generation." His eyes swept over our little group. "A new era is coming. Join me, please, next Saturday night, to celebrate the dawn."

"You mean . . ." Delia's eyes sparkled in the dusky light. "We're going to party at your place?"

Dag tossed his head. "That's right, sweetheart."

"Dag, darling, how exciting." Even my aunt sounded star-struck.

I clapped along with the rest of them.

"Ready, everybody?" Dag smashed a hand against the strings, and I jumped at the thundering sound. "For the new world?" In the firelight, his scar slashed red across his cheek.

He smiled at me. "It's time for Dag Ashton and Cyclone!" He leaped up and strutted around the firepit to the beat of his guitar. He loomed over me now, like a tall, dark crag of rock. He threw his head down and back, whipping his black hair into the air. "How about it, Tory? Will you come with me into the new era?"

My mouth dropped open as I stared at him.

The guitar blasted, and he lunged toward me, then sprang back, hurling his guitar up and down as he sang. "Consumed by fi-yer . . . ravenous ritual . . . powerful fire . . . Take me unaware . . . Take me anywhere . . . Burn . . . Burn . . ."

I tried to jerk my eyes from his, but all I could see was Dag and the flames behind him. "Bright as burning night . . . Full of potent light . . . Burn . . . Burn . . ." He howled words about fire. Over and over. Louder and louder.

"Burn . . . Burn . . ." His voice soared to a wail. "Give me your power . . . I'll give you everything in return . . . Come on, Tory . . . Burn . . . Burn . . ."

All I could smell was smoke.

All I could feel was fire.

Memories exploded in my mind.

So hot! So much smoke! Mom! Dad! Where are you?

I leaped up and ran across the patio.

CHAPTER

FOUR

My bare feet pounded on cold sand. I raced to the ocean and dipped my hands in the foam, splashing my burning cheeks. My sword swung out and brushed against my chin. It felt hot, as if it glowed with fiery light.

The salt air felt clean in my lungs. My heart slowed. The death terrors faded. The fire was over. But it was too late for Mom and Dad. The firemen had carried me out of the burning house, and I'd never seen them again.

I leaped up and ran along the beach. Tears and seawater cooled my cheeks. My feet slapped against the sand.

A voice shouted over the roar of the waves.

"Tory." Greg ran up beside me. His hair caught the moonlight in a ribbon of gold.

"I'm not going back." I wiped my cheeks.

He touched my arm. "Why did you take off?"

"That song! Fire's not beautiful! How could he say that? It's horrible!"

"I know, kid." He looked at me. "Dag didn't mean to upset you. The song's about passion, not real fire. If he knew about your parents, he'd never have sung that song tonight."

"He's a horrible person, Greg. And he hates me!"

His brown eyes softened. "No way. He always looks mean when he sings. His rock image, you know?"

"No." I sprinted away.

"Hold on." Greg ran alongside me.

At the north end of the cove, a wall of rock rose in front of us. I kicked the sand. No way out.

I spun around, walking fast. Greg stayed beside me. Fireworks sprayed into the sky above the black house.

Our footsteps slowed, and I took a deep breath. "My aunt likes Dag, doesn't she?"

"We all do."

"I don't know if I do . . ." I remembered the way he looked at me when he sang. Ferocious. Like a wild animal ready to rip me to shreds. "I know he's a rock star and everything, but what else makes everybody like him?"

"He cares."

"About people?"

"About his neighbors. About the coast. After he built his house, he organized the families at the cove. He put up half the money and talked us into buying the land so no one else could build here." He stopped and looked down at me. "Lots of people say they're concerned about the coastline, but Dag spends his money to prove it."

"And that makes him a hero?"

"In a way. A lot of beaches have been wrecked by developers. Dag saved Rock Cove. All of us are grateful to him."

"Is that the only reason you like him?"

"He loves the ocean like we do. He's an awesome sailor."

"Oh, yeah? I haven't seen him go out."

"He goes on Tuesdays. Usually by himself.

41

Once in awhile, he takes one of the neighbors out. He's got a great Hobie Cat."

"Have you gone out with him?"

"Sure." He smiled. "That Cat can really rip."

"Does Elissa go too?"

"No. She's always painting. Hey, look!" He pointed out over the ocean. A shower of stars lit the sky, shooting out trails of red and gold that shone in the water. Muffled strains of rock music floated out to the sand.

"She never talks, does she?"

He shook his head. "Since her mom died, she hasn't said a word."

"You mean she can't talk even if she wants to?"

"I guess not. She just draws."

"Yeah," I said, thinking of the picture she'd done of me. Until I'd seen that sketch in front of my eyes, I'd thought of my sword as a symbol. A symbol of good. But she'd drawn it as a weapon. And me as a warrior. It had startled me, but I kind of liked that drawing. Maybe if I asked her for it, she'd give it to me. "I feel sorry for her. Not pity, or anything, because I have a feeling she's strong inside. But I can tell she's been through a lot."

"She sure has." We walked, and Greg's arm brushed mine. "Her mom's death was hard on her."

"Does she have any friends?" I asked.

"Not that I know of. I've tried to talk to her a few times, but she doesn't seem interested."

"She must be lonely." I tried to imagine growing up in that horrible house, but I couldn't.

"I think she wants it that way. All she likes to do is draw and paint."

"How could anyone want to be alone all the time?" I thought of Amy and Taylor and how much I missed them, and all my friends back home.

"I don't know, but some people do."

"Not me." I shivered.

"Hey, you're cold." Greg put his arm around me, and I leaned against him, breathing in the damp wooly scent of his sweater, and getting a whiff of his shampoo, like herbs in a garden.

Waves tumbled to shore in soft thuds. Above us, stars decorated the sky like diamonds on black velvet. The Big and Little Dippers glowed in the heavens, reminding me of happier times.

"Greg . . ."

"Yeah?"

"When you were little, did you wish on stars?"

"I still do. Don't tell anybody."

I smiled up at him. "What do you wish for?"

"I don't know. The perfect wave, to build my own house by the ocean, stuff like that. What about you?"

"I used to wish for a gold medal in gymnastics, but now . . ." What could I say? That I wished for the impossible, for my life to be whole again? Or even the possible, the wish I didn't dare say, that I wished for a boyfriend like him? Suddenly the night seemed darker and wider to me. "I wish the sun would stay out all summer," I said quickly.

"You're a funny kid, you know that?"

"Yeah." Guys always thought of me as a kid. I pulled myself up tall.

Greg's brown eyes shone in the moonlight. "You've really got guts, Tory. Moving out here by yourself and everything. I admire that."

"Thanks." I was glad he thought I was brave, even though I knew better. But I'd rather he thought I was sexy.

"Ready to go back?" he asked. "My truck's in the shop, and I've got to get up before dawn to catch the Greyhound. I'm heading back to L.A. for the week."

I looked down at the sand, dark and clammy under my bare feet. "Not really."

"Come on." He touched my arm. We walked over the dunes and crossed the road to the patio.

I said goodnight to Greg and his mom and watched them stroll up the road toward their house. Aunt Julia and Dr. Krieger moved around the patio, straightening furniture and clearing dishes. Delia was nowhere in sight.

Dag and Elissa crossed the patio and stopped beside me at the gate. Dag's eyes glowed like two silver coins in the dim light. "I've never had anyone abandon a performance, Tory. Did my singing disturb you?"

"I hate songs about fire." I told him coldly. How could he be so selfish? Someone must have explained about my parents.

"I wrote *Consumed By Fire* for Elissa." His long fingers curled around her shoulder. "She understands that fire is nothing to fear. She is part of the new era."

45

"What new era?"

"The era of oneness, Tory. The dawn of pure power. Without Elissa, all my hopes and dreams would die. Truth would die." He squeezed her thin shoulder, and the ring on his finger glittered against her blouse.

His words hung between us like strange signs in a foreign language. I wondered what it would be like to have Dag for a father. I thought of Dad, rumpled and normal in his golf sweater and horn-rims, and knew I'd been blessed.

"Elissa," I said. "You know that drawing, the one you did of me with the sword. Can I . . .? I mean, would you give it to me?"

"There's no drawing of you in Elissa's book, Tory." Dag's voice was deep. "She showed me everything she's done tonight."

"Uh . . ." I looked quickly at Elissa who stared down at the ground.

"Okay. Sure. I must be mistaken." But I'd seen it, I knew I had.

Elissa glanced up, and her gray eyes looked so sad that I felt my own eyes burn. She probably missed her mother a lot. I understood. Even though I smiled and said the right things, every time I thought of the fact that I'd never see Mom again, I wanted to run somewhere and howl my head off. Maybe, if we spent some time together, we could help each other to not be so sad. "Would you like to go shell hunting sometime with me, Elissa?" I said impulsively.

A smile flickered across her face, like a breath of wind on a candle flame.

"I'm afraid that's not possible." Dag tightened his hand on her shoulder. "Elissa hasn't been well. She never goes to the beach."

"Why? Did Dr. Krieger say she couldn't?" I asked in a carrying tone, knowing the doctor stood nearby.

Dr. Krieger carefully untied a balloon from the fence. "Actually, Dag, it might be healthy for Elissa to join Tory in a shell hunt."

Dag smiled at him. "Well, Stanley, perhaps you're right. I only want what's best for Elissa." He stroked her long black hair, and she seemed to shrink inward like a flower pulling in its petals. "Maybe I'm overprotective. It's not easy being a single parent."

"How well I know." Dr. K. yanked a red

balloon from the gate, adding it to the bunch in his hand, and smiled at Dag. "But we'll keep forging ahead, won't we?"

"Of course we will, Stanley. I'm lucky I can turn to a professional like you when I need advice. Don't forget. You're sailing with me this Tuesday."

"How could I forget? It's the high point of my week."

"Bring Delia if you wish."

"I don't know, Dag. I think my girl's developed a crush on you, and that worries me."

Dag smiled gently. "I've noticed, but you needn't worry. It goes with the territory in my business. I know how to control the situation without hurting her feelings."

I winced inside. If Delia could hear this conversation, she'd probably bury herself in the sand and not come out for the rest of the summer. I know I would if I were her.

"I'm glad to know that, Dag." Dr. K.'s head bobbed up and down like a wobbly stuffed animal's. "Give me a call if you need to talk."

"I certainly will." Dag smiled as he watched the doctor lumber off.

I fingered my necklace and turned back to Elissa. Her eyes widened suddenly as she stared at my sword. She brought her hand up and moved her fingertips slowly toward my throat.

Dag's hand closed around her wrist before she could reach me. "Time to go, Lissy." He pulled her arm through his and strode through the gate, holding her next to him.

"Dag . . ." Delia pranced down the road toward us. Where's she been hiding, I wondered. "I put your guitar inside your front door like you asked me to." She held out a key.

He grabbed the key without a word and walked past her. Her face crumpled as she watched him march up the road.

Elissa looked over her shoulder at me. Her mouth opened, but no sound came out.

My fingers moved to my sword, and I pressed the familiar shape against my throat.

What had so fascinated Elissa about my necklace? She'd wanted to touch it until Dag stopped her. And why had she thrown away the picture she'd drawn of me before Dag could see it? Or maybe he had seen it and lied. But why would he do that?

Dag and his daughter brought all kinds of questions with them. And when questions didn't have answers, I had to find them.

CHAPTER

FIVE

Groans and moans rose up inside me the next morning as I got out of bed early and forced my body into a series of stretches, then moved into the floor routine that had taken our team to the finals. "Ouch," I cried out in a whisper. "Ooh. Ugh." I was determined to make the team at my new school and show up that snob Delia. You can do it, I kept telling myself. Still, by the time I hit the shower, I felt tight and tense. So much for loosening up.

Downstairs, I slipped onto a stool at the breakfast bar and watched Aunt Julia slide a pan of muffins out of the oven. My mouth tingled at the delicious smell. "Aunt Julia," I said carefully, "I think I'll visit Elissa after breakfast today."

"That might be difficult, darling." My aunt arranged the muffins on a platter, surrounded by strawberries and grapes and slid it onto the breakfast bar. Sun streamed through the window over her shoulder making petals of light on her cotton shirt. "Dag is protective of Elissa. Overly so, in my opinion. But he believes a quiet life, one you or I might even call reclusive, will restore her health, and perhaps she'll talk again."

I grabbed a bran muffin, and held it to my lips a moment, breathing in its sweetness. "How can she talk if she doesn't have anyone to talk to? And why can't she go to the beach? It's mean."

"That's hard for me to understand too." My aunt poured spicy-smelling tea into white mugs. "But Dag is her father and perhaps he knows best. Elissa's a gifted child, but she has emotional problems."

"No wonder, with her mother dying like that." I said, shivering a little. I knew how it felt.

My aunt shoved her glasses up on her nose

and stared at me. "How did you hear about Donna Jean?"

"Greg told me." I picked up my knife carefully. "Why didn't you mention it, Aunt Julia?"

She wrapped a jeweled hand around her mug. Gold rings with winking emeralds glittered on three of her fingers. "I was afraid the tragedy might upset you, darling, and Lord knows you've suffered enough. I was simply appalled last night when Dag sang about fire. He didn't know, of course. Thank heavens Greg saw you leave and followed you."

I straightened my shoulders. "I'm not a baby, Aunt Julia. You don't have to worry about me all the time." Absently, I smoothed butter onto the warm halves of my muffin.

Aunt Julia looked at me steadily. "You're right, Tory. The Madisons are strong stock. We always have been."

I swallowed, wiping crumbs from my lips. Now was as good a time as any to ask what I'd been wondering. "Why did Elissa's mother kill herself?"

"No one knows, really. If only she'd gotten

help, she might be alive today." My aunt sighed. "Donna Jean missed her home town in Tennessee. It was a small, rural place, and she loved it there. She had a terrible time adjusting to the West Coast and the entertainment business."

"Do you really believe she committed suicide because of that?"

"We'll never know for sure. Loneliness can lead one to do desperate things."

"I guess so." Could that be why Elissa was so interested in me, I asked myself. Was she lonely like her mother? Greg said she wanted to be by herself, but I couldn't believe it. I'll be her friend, I decided. Maybe if she had a really good friend, she'd get well and talk again and go to the beach like a normal kid. I needed a friend, too, and kids at Rock Cove weren't exactly lining up for the honor. Greg was terrific, but he was never around, and Delia obviously thought I was the geek of the century. Maybe I could teach Elissa some gymnastics moves. Her small, compact body was perfect for a gymnast.

Aunt Julia sipped her tea. "Now, darling, let's talk about more pleasant subjects. I'm taking you to Beverly Hills today. It's time for a shopping spree. You need clothes."

I nodded. I'd been in a fog when I picked out my clothes for California. Aunt Julia reached across the counter and rummaged around in her pocketbook. "This is for you." She handed me a credit card.

I touched the bumpy numbers with my fingertip. "You don't have to give me this, Aunt Julia. Mom and Dad left some money . . ."

"Hush, darling. Your inheritance is for your college education. Shopping is one of life's lovely extravagances, and so wonderful when you're young and can wear the latest fashions. You have a beautiful figure, Tory. I want you to indulge yourself a little. This is good business training as well. It's never too early to learn about credit."

"Well, okay. Thanks." My name stood out in raised letters on the card. Victoria Madison. *Victorious*. The kids used to call me that at gymnastics meets. They'd chant it before I did my floor exercise, and the yelling and the music would build up inside me, exploding into rolls and roundoffs. I wondered if I could still handle the superior moves.

"You're welcome, darling." She smiled. "By the way, have you decided on changes for your bedroom?"

"I've thought of a few things." I slipped the card in my pocket. "Like pale yellow paint, and wallpaper with blue and yellow flowers, and one of those rugs . . . you know with the patterns like quilts . . ."

"A dhurrie." My aunt smiled. "I see a budding designer before me."

"There's something else, Aunt Julia. I know this is a lot to ask, but one of Elissa's paintings would look so great in my room."

"Darling, what a lovely idea. I'm sure Elissa would be thrilled to do an oil for you."

I smiled. "Thanks, Aunt Julia."

Later that morning, as we drove to the city in my aunt's Mercedes, I made plans. I would ask Elissa to do a seascape, using one of my photos of Cape Cod. My old home. That way, I'd have an excuse to visit her.

Beverly Hills was hot and muggy with a haze of brown tinting the air like leftover smoke. Tall palms swayed in the warm breeze. Shoppers in everything from shorts to sequins strolled along the sidewalks, while traffic roared and honked up the boulevards.

Aunt Julia insisted I try on tons of clothes. I picked out shorts, jeans, sweaters, and a couple of outfits for church. For Dag's party I chose a sexy backless sundress in a turquoise flower print, hoping it made me look mature. After lunch, we browsed in a bookstore. I bought an armload of mysteries, and Aunt Julia got a few cookbooks.

We loaded our shopping bags into the trunk, and as we drove through the city and turned onto the Coast Highway, I stared out at the beach where crowds played volleyball and splashed in the surf. I sighed. Back home, my friends would be doing the usual summer stuff—biking, clamming, and shopping in P-town on the tip of the Cape. I wondered if our sailing club had won the big Fourth of July regatta. Amy and Taylor hadn't mentioned the club in their letters. Maybe they didn't want to remind me of all the fun I was missing.

Eventually, we turned down the winding dirt road to Rock Cove. On the point, the eerie dark house rose from the rocks like a giant tomb. I stared at the jagged walls, and closing my eyes, sent Elissa a message.

I'll see you tomorrow.

CHAPTER

SIX

In the middle of the night, Mom came to me in a dream. She stood on the highest rock of the point, dressed in white, the waves churning around her. Her mouth moved in a soft, sighing whisper.

I strained to hear, but the roar of the waves drowned out her voice. I reached out. If only I could touch her, hold her, but she faded away, turned misty before my eyes. Then it wasn't Mom, but Elissa who held her arms out to me. Her mouth opened, and her lips formed my name. Her mouth was red. So red. And then, I saw bright, red blood splash from her lips onto her white dress. I tried to run, tried to scream, but I couldn't move. She reached for me, and her hands weren't hands at all but ugly lumps of charred flesh.

I woke covered with cold perspiration, choking back a scream. My heart pounded. Outside, the waves moaned. Moonlight filtered through the shutters into my bedroom. I closed my eyes, praying for sleep, but it was no use; the nightmare had brought me wide awake. The rhythm of the waves filled my head like a chant. Hi, low. Hi, low. I buried my head under the pillow, but I couldn't breathe. Pushing back my covers, I climbed out of bed and opened the door to the balcony. Cool air swept into the room. I hugged my arms around my waist, walking out into the darkness. The chanting sound grew louder.

A gold moon gleamed on the wavetops. On the back of the point, a big eucalyptus tree swayed in the breeze near Dag's house. It must be the branches, I thought, making those strange shadows on the ground. I stared hard. The hair stood up on my arms. Those weren't shadows at all, but human shapes! One after another, they came—figures shrouded in dark capes—appearing from the night, gliding toward the black house then vanishing as if they had passed through the walls.

I shrank back against the door and closed my eyes. And then I heard it. A howl that made the blood freeze in my veins. A coyote in the canyon? Or . . . something worse? Taking a deep breath, I forced myself to look back at the point, but all I saw was the big tree waving in the breeze.

Chilled to the bone, I hurried back into bed and pulled the covers up to my chin, feeling my heart race. Scrunching the quilt around my ears, I squeezed my eyes shut and tried to forget my dread. Fear pressed down on me in the dark. I burrowed under the covers. It seemed hours passed before sleep came, and when it did, it was a restless sleep, haunted with bizarre dreams.

It was after eight when I woke the next morning, and I felt like I'd performed in a gymnastics meet during the night. My muscles ached, and my mind felt fuzzy. Wind whistled and shrieked around the house. I thought of the howl I'd heard and wanted to bury myself under the covers again. Instead, I forced myself to work out for an hour, then took a long, hot shower and dressed in a new striped T-shirt and khaki shorts. Maybe Aunt Julia would be in the kitchen baking muffins.

Downstairs, a note waited for me on the breakfast bar. My aunt had an appointment in the city and didn't want to wake me. I nuked a muffin, buttered it, and poured myself a glass of orange juice.

Sunlight bounced off the living room walls, turning them bright as movie screens. Beyond the windows, whitecaps iced the dark blue water, and the wind blew a film of silver sand over the dunes. In the distance, the tip of the black rocks cut into the surf. The place where Mom and Elissa had appeared in my dream. *The place where Donna Jean died.* Suddenly, I wasn't hungry.

I grabbed my jacket and walked out the front door and across the patio. For a minute, I stood there, staring up the road, afraid to take a step toward whatever waited for me in the black house.

The wind howled through the trees,

scattering leaves and scenting the air with a menthol-like smell. I started up the road. Greg's house looked friendly with its welcome plaque on the front door. I passed the blue and white colonial, and kept going. A gust of wind whipped dirt and sand against my legs. Goose bumps popped out on my skin.

I hiked onto the back of the point. The fearsome house towered into the sky, burning my eyes with the glare off its black walls. Eucalyptus branches hurled against each other in the wind, scraping back and forth against stone. Smoke from the chimney blew by me in an acrid cloud.

The strip of land where I stood looked like a long knife blade cutting into the ocean. To my right, a field stretched out, then fell away at cliff's edge into the sea. A black Porsche was parked in the weeds. Dag's?

I made my way along the side of the house toward the front door. A butterfly sailed in front of me onto the black rock, pinned there by the wind, its wings a gold blur that slowed, then stopped, as if the walls had absorbed its life. I scooped the insect up, but it was dead. I squeezed my eyes closed as the feather-soft wings slid from my hand.

Suddenly, the door smashed open, and a short powerfully-built man with wild blond hair stomped out of the house. Kelsey Woodruff! I could feel the energy crackling out of his muscular body.

He jabbed an arm in the air. "It's all over for us Dag! I'll do you a favor, okay? I'm out of Cyclone. You've finally got the lead singer job you always wanted." He stood with his feet planted wide apart, his hands on his hips. "What ever happened to those soft Tennessee sounds, anyway? What ever happened to *Sweet Donna Jean*? Remember that one, Dag? Remember her?"

"I haven't forgotten my wife, Woody." Dag's voice boomed from the doorway. "Or the way you looked at her."

"I could see she was in trouble." Kelsey stood like a broad stump rising from the field. "I have an idea of what you're into, Dag."

"Don't come here again, Woody," Dag growled. "Or you'll be sorry."

"I'm checking up on you when I get back

from Japan. Three weeks. Count on it. You be good to that little girl, or I'll make you regret it." He turned and stalked to the Porsche, leaping over the side into the driver's seat. He fired up the engine, and the car swerved wildly as he tore through the field onto the road.

"You'll crash and burn, Woody." Dag yelled after him. "Without me, you're nothing!" The massive door thudded closed.

I leaned against the wall, breathing fast, feeling the rock stab my back. I should get out of here right now. But something inside me had to know what was going on. Was Elissa in trouble?

Taking a deep breath, I marched to the door and jabbed the doorbell.

CHAPTER

SEVEN

Abruptly, the door swung in. Dag's weird silver-blue eyes swept over me calmly—and coldly. "I had a feeling you'd come, Tory."

My knees trembled. "You did?"

"You're a curious girl, aren't you? One who likes to give destiny a little push?"

I cleared my throat, glancing around the front hall. Aside from the black rock walls, I saw nothing unusual. "Aunt Julia says I may commission a painting from Elissa. That's why I'm here."

"A painting you say?" He threw back his head and laughed. "A creative excuse to intrude. Come in, then." He strode off, leaving me to follow.

I walked quickly after him. An awful smell, like rotten meat charred on a barbeque, filled the air. I swallowed the sick taste that came up in my throat.

The room spiraled out, bigger than the gym at our school. Dag's footsteps echoed across the marble floor. Stone pillars held a balcony three stories high. Statues loomed from every wall and corner. Light filtered in through the domed roof, filling the room with red haze.

I pulled my denim jacket tighter around me. My Reeboks squeaked against the floor, as I passed several purple velvet couches. Dag stood in front of several thick dark tapestries hung next to a fireplace big enough to roast an elephant. Something white lay on top of the burning logs. Something long. A bone? The logs crumbled, and the object diappeared into the burning wood. Above the fireplace was the ugliest thing I'd ever seen. A giant bull's head, its mouth open in a snarl. I walked slowly toward the thing.

"This is Elissa's study time." Dag said. "I can't interrupt her right now. I'm sure you understand."

Not really, I thought. "I can wait for her outside. I won't bother you if you're working or something."

He waved a hand in the air, and the bull's head ring gleamed on his finger. "You're here now, so why don't I give you the grand tour?"

"You don't need to do that."

"Oh, come on. My collection should fascinate an art lover like you." He smiled, and I knew he was mocking me. "The curator at the Malibu Museum was my guest last week. The man could hardly croak out a word, he was so enthralled. Here." He gestured toward a wall to our left. "These are reproductions of ancient masks."

My heart twisted in my chest as I stared at the gaping eye sockets and distorted faces. One mask looked especially fierce, with rings through its ears and nose and a coiled lump on its forehead. They're only clay, I told myself. Nothing to be afraid of.

"Superb, aren't they? These masks were created by the Phoenicians, or Canaanites as you probably know them."

I nodded. I'd heard Dad mention the

Phoenicians lots of times. He'd said they were cruel.

"Over here is a frieze of an ancient sailing ship. The Phoenicians sailed to America twenty-one centuries before Columbus. Did you know that, Tory?"

"No." I put a hand to my nose. The smell was killing me.

"Most people don't." He jerked his head back. "Children don't learn about the ancient cultures in school. That's why I'm home-schooling Elissa." He looked up at the bull's head. "Let me give you a little background.

"Alexander the Great tried to wipe the Phoenicians from the pages of history. He crucified their men and sold their women and children into slavery." He turned and slammed a fist into the wall.

I took a quick step back. What was going on here?

When he faced me again, his eyes glittered. Were those tears? "Alexander wasn't great at all, Tory. He was a sadistic murderer. But he underestimated the strength of this culture." He walked slowly toward me. "Their society was rich, unbelievably rich. The ancient priests knew many mysteries, had many powers. They participated in sacred rites that would shock the 20th century. But they succeeded beyond all reason. Our world could use their talents today."

"Sacred rites?" I remembered the caped figures I'd seen in the middle of the night. "For what?"

"For peace, and so much more. For art, culture, law, commerce. And pleasure. Oh, yes, pleasure." He smiled then moved to the fireplace glancing up at the bull. "This is the Moloch, an ancient Canaanite god."

The bull's teeth glistened with a fiery-red glow. Enormous bronze wings swept above its head, shining in the firelight. Three black stones, bordered by yellow circles formed eyes on its brow. Dag smiled up at the thing. "A god almost forgotten in modern culture. But some remember," he said softly. "The ancients say the gods reside within their images." Dag touched his fingertips to his lips, then reached up and pressed them against the bull.

This is sick. I reached for my sword. It felt tiny between my groping fingers.

Dag looked down at me. "Why do you wear a weapon around your neck, Tory? Are you intrigued with violence?"

"No." I backed up a step. "My parents gave me this. It's a symbol of goodness." My voice sounded weak in the huge room.

He took a step toward me, staring for a long time at my necklace. He smelled so good, like honey, and suddenly I didn't want him to move away.

"It's a beautiful necklace." His voice was deep and rich. "May I see it?"

"I never take it off." I curled my fingers around the sharp little object at my neck, remembering something.

Nothing can harm you in love's circle. Mom had said those words when she fastened the necklace around my neck on my birthday. I smiled inside at the recaptured memory. "Can I see Elissa now?"

"Don't tell me I'm boring you?" His bright-blue eyes mocked me.

"No, but I came here to ask Elissa about the painting."

"Of course." He moved away, and the awful

smell closed in around me again. "Come with me." His footsteps echoed through the hall as he strode to the staircase that spiraled up through the air to the balcony above. I followed him up hundreds of steps, wondering what waited for me.

In the upstairs hall, Dag glanced at his watch. "Elissa will come to her studio soon. You may visit her there." Our feet padded down the dimly-lit hall past arched doors of all different sizes.

We stepped into a room filled with rose-colored light, and I breathed in the clean oil paint smell. One corner held a drafting table and shelves of art supplies. A half-painted seascape of the black rocks rested on an easel. Stacks of canvases, all seascapes like my aunt's, leaned against the walls.

The wind hurled itself at the doors, making them chatter. Dag snatched open a glass door, and cool air swirled around us. He stepped out onto the balcony. "The view out here is the most spectacular in Rock Cove," he said. Wind caught his hair and lifted it in a shining black cloud around his face. "Did you know that the ancient cities of Tyre and Sidon looked out to sea?"

The wind howled around the side of the house. Below us, waves crashed on the rocks. "I love to sail these waters. The coastline is our last treasure. One we have to preserve. Come here. I'll show you the setting of your aunt's seascape."

The place where Donna Jean died. As I stepped over the threshold, the wind whipped up, slamming the door behind us.

Clutching my jacket around me, I walked a few short steps to the balcony's rail where a sheer drop opened over the rocks. Booming waves hurled spray into the air, and a cloudy white dress seemed to hover above the rocks. *Mom, is that you?* Goose bumps prickled along my scalp.

I turned around. Dag faced me, smiling, and his teeth gleamed sharply in the sunlight. "The others leave Elissa and me alone, Tory. They understand we need privacy."

"I just want to be Elissa's friend," I shouted above the wind.

"Elissa has a sacred destiny. No one must interfere." He took a step toward me. "No one."

I tried to move away, but the thin railing cut into my back. Below me, the rocks opened hungry black jaws. The wind blew my hair into my eyes and mouth. I swayed, clutching at the rail.

Then Dag grabbed my arms.

CHAPTER

EIGHT

I screamed.

A gust of wind swept the hair from my eyes. Behind Dag, a white figure appeared at the glass doors.

"Elissa!" I cried.

Dag pulled me away from the rail. "What's the matter, Tory? Afraid of heights? There's nothing to worry about. You're safe with me." He pulled me under his arm, drew me toward the glass doors. The honey-smell surrounded me. I relaxed against him.

Elissa and I stared at each other as Dag led me inside. My teeth clicked together, and I clenched my jaw to stop the shaking.

Dag let go of me. "Have you finished your reading so soon, Lissy?"

She nodded, holding out a large book. I glanced at the title. "Children of Sacrifice." Her eyes darted to me.

"Tory has come to commission a painting," Dag said. "Go ahead. Tell my daughter what you want."

My head filled with an image of me wielding a sword against an unknown enemy. "Can I be alone with her for a minute to talk about it?"

"I'm afraid not. Elissa only has a short break. Then, it's back to the books." His smile was gentle. "If you'd called first, Tory, maybe there would have been time."

"I can come back later."

"Not today."

Why can't we be alone now, I wanted to scream. Was Elissa a prisoner in her own house? I remembered the butterfly trapped on the wall. She stared at me, and I forced a smile. "I'd like you to paint a seascape for me, Elissa." I reached into my pocket and brought out a photo of our beach on Cape Cod. "Will you paint this scene?"

She studied it, and her delicate mouth curved into a smile. She nodded. Her eyes met mine, and I sensed they held secrets she wanted to share with me. If only we could be alone.

"The painting will be ready Saturday night," Dag said, putting his arm around Elissa. "You may pick it up at my party. You'll be coming with Julia?"

"Yes. But how can she finish it so quickly?"

"She will." He smiled at his daughter. "She is supernaturally gifted."

Elissa looked at the ground.

Dag moved toward the hall. "I'll see you out, Tory."

Elissa's fingers pressed mine, then let go.

I turned. "If it's not ready by Saturday," I whispered, "it's okay."

She pressed her fingertips against her lips, shaking her head. I wanted to ask her about the sketch she'd done of me, but her eyes begged me not to say more.

I touched her arm. "Bye, Elissa." I followed Dag down the long staircase, staring straight ahead, trying not to breathe the rotten charred smell.

He threw open the front door, and I rushed toward it. "Elissa's destiny was determined before time," Dag called after me. "One small girl is powerless to change it."

"I don't know what you're talking about," I told him. Wind swept into the room, as if to pull me from the house, and I slipped past him. He was crazier than I thought.

He laughed softly. "You will before the summer is over." The door thudded behind me.

Back in my room, I tried to read. But the words blurred in front of my eyes. I shoved a tape into my cassette player, and as guitar music throbbed into the room, I bent over and flattened my palms on the floor. My limbs were becoming more resiliant. Good. I'd missed being in shape. I stretched for awhile then practiced backbends and splits, trying to work out the tension in my body and clear my head. Why wouldn't Dag let me talk to Elissa, I wondered. I wasn't exactly one of those kids who sent parents screaming into the night. You'd think he'd want his daughter to have friends. But maybe he really thought she was better off staying quiet. I didn't believe it, though, and it made me mad.

Use your emotion in the moves, my coach always said. I hurtled through an old floor routine, working out my feelings in explosions of energy that just kept coming. Thank goodness this bedroom was huge. Had Dag meant me harm on that balcony, I wondered, or was I being paranoid? *Let it go*, I told myself. *Let it out*. I flew into a set of flawless cartwheels. I couldn't make a wrong move, and when I finally collapsed on the bed, I was shocked to see how late it was.

I didn't talk or eat much dinner that night. Aunt Julia was quieter than usual too. After strawberries and ice cream, we settled in front of the smooth granite fireplace, me with my mystery and my aunt with stacks of building plans.

I opened my book, but all I could see was Elissa's wide gray eyes. What did she want from me? Across the room, my aunt sat with her legs curled under her on the sofa. Her eyes moved back and forth over the plans. Dad used to get those same two lines between his eyebrows when he studied. I let my book drop into my lap. I'd always been able to talk to Dad about anything.

"Aunt Julia, I'm worried about Elissa," I said.

Her eyes met mine. She slid her glasses off and rubbed the bridge of her nose. "I'm sorry, darling. I'm afraid I'm rather preoccupied. My client, a man from New York, wants the impossible. Forgive me. What was it you said?"

I moved to the edge of the couch. "I went over to Dag's today, to ask about my painting. We were on the balcony. He came toward me . . ." My fingers closed around my book. "I don't know what he was going to do."

"What do you mean?" She leaned forward, scrunching her elbows into the stack of papers.

"I got dizzy and scared. It was the height, or maybe it was Dag. I'm not sure. I know he doesn't want me to see Elissa."

My aunt sighed and leaned back on the sofa. "I'm not surprised. Stan—you know, Dr. Krieger—and I have tried to talk to Dag about his overprotectiveness, but he doesn't seem to understand."

"Something's weird over there, Aunt Julia. Dag called this awful bull over his fireplace a god. And there were horrible masks on the walls." My stomach rolled over as I remembered the rancid smell and the white thing in the fireplace.

Aunt Julia slipped on her glasses. "Dag's art collection is a bit intimidating if one isn't used to such things. The occult has never been one of my favorite subjects, either." She set the stack of paper beside her on the sofa. "Like many musicians, Dag is rather eccentric. But he's a generous neighbor."

"I know. He bought the land and everything."

"Yes. He adored Donna Jean, and her death deeply affected him. Unfortunately, Elissa has suffered because of their tragedy. After Donna Jean died, I suggested that Elissa stay with me temporarily, but he wouldn't hear of it. He's a southerner through and through and would rather offer hospitality than accept it."

"Does anyone know for sure how Donna Jean died? Did she really kill herself? Or did somebody push her off that balcony?"

"Tory!" My aunt looked shocked. "What a thing to suggest!" She glanced at the book in my lap. "Too many mysteries, perhaps?"

"No!" I leaped up, and the paperback tumbled to the floor.

"Oh, Tory . . ." Aunt Julia was next to me, her arms around me. "You've been through a terrible ordeal. No wonder you're feeling threatened."

I pulled away. "It's not that."

She patted my arm. "Everyone at the cove understands Dag. You will too, in time. Sometimes his concern for Elissa is obsessive, but he would never physically harm her."

I bent stiffly to pick up my book. This wasn't like talking to Dad. "I think I'll go up to my room, Aunt Julia. I'm tired."

"All right, darling." I felt her worried eyes on me as I climbed the stairs.

In my room, I undressed and stepped into the shower. In spite of the pounding hot water, my body ached from tension, or maybe from my long workout. The spray needled into my skin. Suddenly, I felt silly.

Dag was strange, sure. But there was no law

against being strange. This was California, after all. Things were different here. So he collected ugly ancient art. So he talked about destiny all the time. I had to calm down. What had happened to the cool, sensible person I used to be? Dad always said I was the pragmatist of the family. He called me Ms. *Logic* and said if there were a question, I'd find the answer to it.

But the way I felt about Dag wasn't logical. I stepped out of the shower and rubbed a towel hard over my skin. If only Dad were here now. He might know about Moloch. Thinking of that bull's head, I shivered. Dag was the weirdest person I'd ever met. I didn't know whether I liked him or hated him. I remembered how I'd followed him out to the balcony like a lovesick puppy. *Never again* I swore to myself as I pulled on my new lavender sleepshirt with the turquoise palm trees on the front.

Outside, waves crashed on the shore. I thought of the shadowy figures I'd seen in the middle of the night. What would Aunt Julia say about them? That I'd had a nightmare?

I only wished I could be sure I had.

CHAPTER

NINE

On Wednesday, a carton arrived for me from the university. The chairman of the Theology Department had mailed the stuff from Dad's office. I pulled out Dad's gold pen and pencil set and a golf trophy. The shiny gold statue felt cold and smooth under my fingers. I remembered how excited he'd been to win the tournament. It had been some charity benefit—I couldn't remember which.

Next was a framed picture of Mom and me standing by our Christmas tree. Was it only a few months ago that I'd stood there with nothing on my mind but opening presents? It seemed like another girl who laughed out at the camera. A girl who expected life to go on forever the way it was then. How dumb could you get?

I dusted off the picture and set it on the bureau, trying to imagine what Mom would tell me now. Maybe she'd remind me that as long as I wore my sword, I'd be safe. But Dad said the sword was a weapon. To fight for good. Was I supposed to use it? To fight what? Dad had told me that sometimes the enemy was a spiritual force that you couldn't see. If you couldn't see it, how could you fight it?

I shoved the carton of books into my closet to look through later. I couldn't stop thinking about Elissa. No bruises or marks marred her white skin, but something was wrong. I knew Dag didn't treat her right. I'd have to get hard evidence to convince my aunt, though. I'd have to be Ms. *Logic*.

By the time Saturday night arrived, I'd come up with a plan. At Dag's party I'd find a way to be alone with Elissa. Dag would be too busy playing host to be with her every second. I'd try to find out if she was unhappy or scared. I found a small writing tablet and pencil and slipped them into the pocket of my sundress. She couldn't talk, but she could write.

The night was clear and balmy. Aunt Julia suggested we walk, and when we arrived, at least fifty cars filled the field next to Dag's house. Rock music gushed through the doorway like a roaring waterfall. I wrinkled my nose as we walked through the hall. A sweet smell filled the house, as if everything was drenched in maple syrup. Dag had really poured on the incense tonight.

A stage had gone up in the main room, where the Cyclone Band pounded on guitars, keyboard, and drums. It looked like four Dags up there with their dark clothes and long hair. Red light splattered over the guests, who danced wildly to the pounding beat.

Dag strode up to us wearing a dark red shirt and leather pants. "Welcome, Julia and Tory." He kissed my aunt's hand. "Julia, I've begun arrangements for the benefit concert for the coast. As soon as Cyclone returns from touring."

"That's wonderful news, Dag." She smiled up at him.

He turned to me. "Your painting is ready, Tory. You'll find it in the closet near the front door."

I took a deep breath. "Where's Elissa? I want to thank her."

"Elissa?" He raised an eyebrow. "She's far too delicate to be out in a crowd like this."

"Where is she?"

"Safe, Tory." He touched my arm, and I pulled away from his cool fingers.

Delia strode up to us, slipping her arm through Dag's. Her blond hair glowed pink under the lights.

"Hello Delia," my aunt greeted her. "Is your father here?"

"Yes." She never took her eyes from Dag's face, and when she spoke her voice was dreamy. "He's here somewhere."

"Enjoy yourselves." Dag turned and sauntered off with the tall blond girl hanging on his arm.

Aunt Julia stared at them for a second before turning to me. "Why don't we find Stan, darling?"

"You go ahead, Aunt Julia."

"Will you be all right?"

"Sure." I smiled determinedly. "I want to watch the dancers."

"Well, if you're certain . . . I won't be long." She floated off through the crowd.

I patted the pad and pencil in my pocket. Elissa must be upstairs. The stairway was in semi-darkness. I glanced across the room. Dag stared at me over Delia's head. I looked away. *Later. When the time is right.*

Dancers whirled around me, and a woman bumped me as she whizzed by. Her hair was slicked into a black ponytail on the side of her head. She wore white makeup and what looked like black lipstick and a silver mini-skirt. I smiled thinking of what Amy and Taylor would say.

"You look happy, kid. Don't tell me. You found a black abalone!" Greg grinned at me from the edge of the dance floor. He looked fantastic in faded jeans and a white muslin shirt with the sleeves rolled up. His sun-streaked hair gleamed red under the lights.

My heart did a major flip. "No. I don't know, I just feel good, I guess."

He gazed intently at me. "That's a good-looking dress."

"Thanks." I smoothed back my hair. Why couldn't it behave for once? "Do you know anybody here?" Dancers twirled and dipped around us.

Greg shook his head. "They look familiar though. Could be the cast from *Night of the Living Dead*."

I laughed. "And we're the last two normal humans on earth."

"Yeah." He looked around. "Have you seen Delia?"

"Over there. Near the fireplace." She was plastered to Dag's side. He had one arm draped around her shoulders, and when he looked down at her, his eyes shone like stars in a midnight sky. I caught my breath. Just for a moment, I wanted to be in her place.

"Dag's helping her with her acting," Greg said. "Introducing her to people."

"Really? I didn't know Delia was an actress."

"Yeah. She performs in all the school plays."

"And she wants to do it professionally?"

"She's already done some commercials and bit parts, but she can't seem to get a foot in the big-time door. All she needs is a break."

"And Dag can get it for her?"

"He promised her he would. When she's ready."

I wondered when that would be. "You really like her a lot, huh?"

"Truth, Tory?"

"Sure, truth."

"I love Dee more than I like her."

My heart crashed like a body to the mat.

"We've known each other since we were two. But I can't get close to her anymore. Delia's out for herself. Know what I mean?"

"I think so." My heart was slowly recovering. "Why don't you show me the stuff you built for Dag?"

"Okay. Over here." I followed him to the wall behind the stage. Pounding drums shook the house.

He pointed, then leaned down to shout in my ear. "I designed and built the shelves and did most of the wood trim in the house. Dag asked me to build a stage upstairs in the sound room. But I promised your aunt I'd paint and paper your room first."

"Great!" I shouted. The wooden shelves glowed with a soft, burnished light. "You do fine work, Greg."

"Glad you like it. Julia told me I should be an architect. I'm considering the idea."

"Sounds good. By the way, where's your mom tonight?"

"She flew back east to meet my dad. My sister lives in Connecticut, and they'll be staying with her for awhile."

The band launched into *Sweet Donna Jean*.

Greg smiled at me. "Want to dance?"

"Sure." I slipped my hand in his, and we walked to the dance floor. He opened his arms. The angels are with me, I thought. It's a slow dance. I moved next to him.

The singer had a husky tenor voice, not as good as Dag's but okay. "Sweet Donna Jean . . . Sweet Donna Jean . . . Eyes as blue as a mountain stream . . ." I wondered about Donna Jean and all the dreams she must have had and the awful way she died, and I felt sad. But when I looked up at Greg, all I could think about was the two of us. I rested my head on his shoulder, and the other dancers faded away. Greg's shirt felt soft against my cheek, his hands warm and strong on my back. I breathed in the fresh scent of his after-shave, wishing the song would go on forever.

We weaved in and out of the other couples, and just as I had us going steady in my mind, the music exploded. Greg spun me out, and I bounced into the steps that had earned me some fame as a dancer at my old school. Greg laughed. His body was lithe, powerful as he moved to the beat, every muscle under perfect control, just like when he surfed. His hair flopped over his forehead. I matched him move for move, looking up into his brown eyes. My gymnastics practice was paying off. I moved like a well-oiled machine.

The fast songs kept coming, but it seemed like we'd only danced for a second when the band announced they were taking a break. Greg twirled me. "You're a good dancer, you know that?"

"So are you." I pushed back my hair.

"I'm starving. Let's get something to eat."

He held my hand as we walked to the buffet table laid out with platters of food and a huge pyramid of fruit.

A sucking sound came from the fireplace. Two men in black shirts yanked a giant slab of meat off a spit and slapped it on the biggest silver platter I'd ever seen. They jammed knives into the hunk of flesh, and bloody juice spurted onto steel blades. The black, crackling skin smelled burned. I remembered the white thing in the fireplace. My stomach squeezed.

"How about some venison steak?" Greg picked up a silver plate. "You know. Deer meat."

I shook my head. "No, thanks."

I served myself rice, vegetables, and fruit. Firelight glared off the bronze bull into my eyes. I looked up at Greg. "Has Dag told you about his statues, Greg? That bull, I mean?"

Greg shook his head, chewing. "No, but he knows I'm bored with that kind of stuff." He looked away, and I could tell he was searching for Delia. He still cared about her, maybe more than he knew, but I really didn't think he liked her as a girlfriend anymore. Across the room, she stood with Dag as he talked to a couple of bearded guys. Bigwigs in the music business, I guessed.

I glanced at the staircase. A noisy crowd milled over the bottom steps. A guy with a brown ponytail leaped up and ran across the room onto the stage. The rest of the band appeared behind him, and the drummer gave a long roll. "Get ready," he yelled. "To meet the new Cyclone!"

Dag strode through the crowd and bounded onstage. Sweeping up his guitar, he turned to scowl at us, his eyes steel blue in the hazy light. A hush fell on the crowd.

"It's time, everybody!" His gravelly voice echoed through the room. "Time for an era where fire burns bright. Where all people learn to do right!" He slammed a hand into his guitar, and the chords thundered off the walls.

"Yes, Dag!" a girl in front of me screamed. "Yes!" Cries broke out over the audience.

He bent backward, swinging his guitar in the air. "Let Cyclone sweep you inside!" The drums crashed to life. The guitars soared. He leaped to the edge of the stage and crouched there, staring out at us. "Are you ready for Dag? Are you really ready?"

The crowd roared.

He strutted along the front of the stage, jerking his head up and down as he growled the lyrics. Around me, people went wild.

I squeezed Greg's hand and looked up at him. "I'll be back," I mouthed.

He nodded.

I plowed through the pack of people like a swimmer through heavy surf.

A cheering group blocked the stairway. I twisted through the partyers, taking a quick look back at Dag. He marched across the stage, hurling words at his screaming fans.

I started up the stairs.

CHAPTER

TEN

I crept up the giant staircase, moving quickly through the dim light. Behind me, the hall wound into blackness. The doorknob of Elissa's studio turned under my hand, and inside, faint moonlight eased the darkness. Nothing had changed except the canvas on the easel, another painting of the black rocks. I backed into the hall, moving to the next door.

"Elissa!" I pressed my ear to the wood. Frenzied music came from downstairs. Yells throbbed with the drums. I rapped sharply, then listened. Nothing.

"Elissa." I knocked again. "Are you in there?"

The music broke. A rustling sound came from behind the door. Splinters of red light flicked across the wood as my cheek pressed its smooth surface. I rapped again. "It's me, Tory. Can I come in?"

A knock answered me.

The knob slipped through my hands. Locked! I glanced at the crack under the door. Taking the pad and pencil from my pocket, I shoved them into the opening. "Write me a note. Quick. Tell me if something's wrong," I scribbled. The pad and pencil disappeared from sight. I glanced over my shoulder into the empty hall. Downstairs, the music throbbed to life, and cheers filled the air. A piece of paper appeared under the door. Not from my tablet, from a sketch book. I picked up the paper and stared at it.

Seconds went by before I could take in what I saw there. Sketched on the paper was a bull's head. Its jaws gaped in a snarl and fire roared from its mouth and nostrils. I swallowed hard. A girl was trapped in its jaws, her dress in flames, her mouth opened in a scream. The girl was Elissa. At the paper's right edge, a hand

97

held a sword pointed at the bull. My hand? Rock music swelled to drown out my thumping heart. What could the picture mean?

A soft thud came nearby. A footstep? I looked up and nearly passed out from pure terror. Dag stood there, staring down at me.

"Hello, Tory." His voice washed over me like icy water.

I shrank against the door, holding the sketch behind my back, my heart hammering against my ribs.

He folded his arms. "Tell me something. What would you call a party guest who invades her host's privacy?"

"I just . . . Why can't Elissa come to the party?"

"Oh, come on. I've explained that to you. Elissa can't mix with this crowd."

"Or any crowd?"

"What did you say?"

I cleared my throat. "There are other kids here."

"Their parents are too permissive. Elissa is my responsibility, and I see now that you need my protection, too."

98

"No I don't."

He smiled. "Don't worry, Tory. I'll take good care of you." He raised his hand, and the big ring glowed with red light as if melting into his fingers. A sweet scent drifted around me. Like honey. Like sunshine. Like every beautiful thing I'd ever smelled. My arms relaxed at my sides. My neck felt wobbly, and all I could see were his silver-blue eyes.

"Come now."

I couldn't pull my eyes from his. Inside those silver-blue orbs lived worlds I could only imagine. Exotic worlds. Mysteries I would give anything to understand.

"Give me the sketch, Tory." He held out his hand.

I shook my head.

"Then I'm afraid Elissa will have to pay for your disobedience."

"No."

"Every action has its consequence."

The sketch dangled from my fingers.

"That's a good girl." He grabbed the paper and crumpled it in his fist.

I felt his hand cup my elbow, and it was as if

I floated away from the door. His voice came from far above me. "You can't fight destiny, Tory."

A rushing sound filled my ears. He took my hand and led me to the stairway. I could barely feel my legs move as we walked downstairs and plunged into the widly dancing crowd. Music blasted into us. "Dag!" A woman reached for him.

I looked around. Where was he? I took a step and stumbled into someone. My head throbbed with the drums. My knees felt like rubber. And then I heard him singing. Back onstage. I felt so desolate, like I'd lost something terribly important.

"Tory!" Dr. Krieger took my arm. "You look pale, my dear. How about some fresh air?"

"Okay." I let Dr. K. lead me out the massive door between cars across the field to the cliff. Below us, moonlight squiggled on the black water. I breathed the cool, salty air. We stood there for a long time, looking out at the ocean. The night air cleared my head. I felt as if I'd awakened from a dream.

"How are you feeling now?" He wore a yellow shirt and dark-green bow tie. His amber eyes looked worried.

"Fine, Dr. Krieger."

"Stan, Tory. Call me Stan."

"Stan." I took a deep breath.

"You looked like you were going to faint. Did you eat something tonight?"

"Yes. I'm okay now." But Elissa wasn't. I knew it now. "I need to ask you something."

"Of course."

"Being a doctor, you know a lot about people, right?"

He smiled. "Hopefully, a little. Although my daughter tells me otherwise."

"I need to ask you something about Dag. Well, not Dag but Elissa. Is something wrong with her?"

"Elissa?" He reached up and fingered his bow tie. "My opinion is that she hasn't grieved properly for her mother. There are certain steps one must go through to heal from such a loss. Why do you ask?"

"Well, because . . ." I waved my arm toward the house. "She's locked in her room right now. She can't even come to the party. Dag says he's protecting her."

"Hmm, I'm afraid, Tory, I must concur with

Dag. It *is* an unruly crowd to subject an unstable young girl to."

"But that's not fair!"

"Perhaps not."

"Hey, you two." Greg stood at the edge of the field. "See you later. Got to get some sleep." He strolled up the road, and I watched him until he disappeared in the dark.

I turned back to Dr. Krieger. "I'm afraid Elissa's going to get hurt. I think Dag is into some creepy cult. He talks about ancient rituals and supernatural powers."

The doctor frowned. "Rituals? What kind of rituals?"

"I don't know. He calls the bull over the fireplace Moloch. Have you heard of it? He says it's a god."

"No. I have not heard of Moloch, but Dag's artistic taste runs to the unusual."

"It's not just art. Elissa gave me something tonight. A sketch she'd made of the bull. The thing's mouth was on fire. Elissa was inside. And she was screaming." I pressed my eyes with my fingertips.

"Do you have the sketch?" Dr. Krieger asked.

"No."

"Where is it?"

"I gave it to Dag."

He raised an eyebrow.

"If I hadn't, Elissa would be in trouble."

"I see." He paused. "You must understand, Tory, that Elissa has emotional problems. I suppose you've noticed that she's obsessed with painting the rocks where Donna Jean died."

"Why won't someone help her?"

"Dag and I had a long discussion on our sailing jaunt. He promised he would find psychiatric treatment for her in Tennessee, while she is visiting her grandparents. They leave Wednesday, so it won't be long until she receives the help she needs."

My heart turned cold. I'd forgotten Elissa was leaving in four days. "Do you think he's telling the truth?"

"Oh, yes. I think so. Dag loves his daughter."

Does he, I wondered. Dag seemed to have charmed everyone at Rock Cove into thinking he was an incredible guy. And everything creepy about him seemed to have a logical explanation. "I hope you're right."

I followed Dr. K. into the house, and we were quickly separated in the frenzy of dancers. I will not party with Elissa a prisoner upstairs, I thought, even if it is supposedly for her own good. I stared into the crowd. Where was my aunt? I had to find her and get the house keys. I had to go home.

Dancers spun around the floor, hurling themselves in time with the music. In the red glare they looked like the masks come to life, eyes and mouths open wide, bodies spinning, blurring before my eyes.

An elbow slammed into my arm. I flinched, stepped back and was whipped in the face by a girl's long dark hair. I felt a sting on my neck and reached up to touch my charm. *Nothing there!* I grasped at the back of my neck, my throat, brushed my hand over my chest.

Frantically, I looked around me. The dancers leered at each other, their feet a stomping tangle against the floor. My eyes swept the crowd. No one I knew. Panic swept through me.

My necklace was gone!

CHAPTER

ELEVEN

I twisted through the dancing bodies, desperate to spot a glint of gold on the floor, yelling questions at people, but no one heard me. I found Aunt Julia, and we looked everywhere, but stomping feet covered most of the floor. After an hour of searching, my aunt insisted we go home. In the entry hall, she opened the closet and pulled out my wrapped painting.

At home in my room, I was too upset to unwrap the canvas. A hollow place had opened up inside me from the moment my necklace disappeared. I pulled on pajamas and brushed my teeth. As I climbed under the covers, Aunt

Julia came in and tucked my quilt around me. "Your necklace will turn up, darling. Have faith."

"I'm trying to." I squeezed my eyes closed and felt hot tears. It was the last thing I had left of my parents.

"I want you to remember something, Tory." Aunt Julia pressed her cheek to mine. "I love you, darling. Very much." Her skin was warm and soft, and her hair tickled my nose. Her perfume, faded now, smelled musky. "Sleep well, my child."

"I love you, too, Aunt Julia," I whispered. I could never love my aunt the way I'd loved Mom and Dad, but I really liked her, and that was a kind of love, wasn't it?

She kissed me on the forehead and crossed the room to flick off the light.

Alone in the dark, a terrible heaviness crushed down on me, as if I'd lost Mom and Dad all over again. Please God, I prayed, if you won't bring back Mom and Dad, at least bring back their gift to me. Some people said you weren't supposed to pray for things like that, but I always told God how I felt. The clock on the bedside table ticked off the hours, as I lay there blinking in the dark. The ceiling seemed to press lower and lower until I couldn't breathe. Finally, I reached over and flicked on the light. Across the room, my painting leaned against the bureau. I padded over and tore off the brown paper, taking a deep breath as the canvas appeared.

So beautiful, I thought. The long white beach on the Cape. Would I ever walk there again? I pressed my forehead to the canvas and felt the rough texture of paint against my skin. If only I could vanish into that scene, hunt shells along that shore, I'd be happy.

Without thinking, I reached **up** to touch my sword, seeking the link to my parents, but found only bare skin. I wrapped my arms around my knees. You have to concentrate, I told myself. Where is it? The last time I'd been aware of the gold chain around my neck was when I bent down to shove the tablet under Elissa's door. After that, I'd gone outside with Dr. Krieger. What if I'd dropped it in the field? My heart squeezed as I thought of the cars leaving the party. But even if my sword were smashed, I wanted it. If I waited until tomorrow morning, the sun would reflect off the gold. A curious gull might carry it off. Then I'd never find it.

I tore off my pajamas and yanked on sweats. A flashlight lay tucked in my top drawer. I grabbed it and tiptoed out of my room. My aunt's light was out. I didn't wake her.

The full moon guided me up the road. I crept across the field to the cliff where Dr. Krieger and I had talked, working my way slowly back toward the house with my flashlight. Far below, waves murmured on the shore. The air had turned cold and damp. I aimed my light at the weeds, most of which were smashed flat. I stayed in the area Dr. Krieger and I had covered, feeling along the ground with my hands. Nothing!

As the surf swept back into the sea, a deep, insistent roll of sound filled the night air. I glanced at the house. Red light filtered through a crack where the front door stood ajar. I listened carefully. High, low. High, low. Chanting. My heart sped up. Something was going on in there. Bending low, I turned off my flashlight and crept toward the door.

The eerie noises swelled as I neared the house. My foot caught on a something hard. I went down. The flashlight tumbled away. My hands and knees stung. I looked around me. Moonlight glinted on steel. I grabbed the flashlight and shoved it into my sweatshirt, and then, I froze.

A caped figure glided along the side of the house. I held my breath. Closer, closer, it came, then stopped. The figure turned toward the door, pushing it open. Something long and black hung over its arm. Voices rose inside. The sounds took form. "Moloch. Moloch. Moloch." The hood on the cape slipped, and I caught a glimpse of blond hair. Delia? The door boomed shut. Then, there was only the sound of the waves.

I crouched in the grass, waiting, but no one came in or out of the house. Dampness soaked through my sweatshirt, and my teeth chattered in the frigid night air. Then it came. A sound so horrible that it made the hair stand up all over my body. I knew that sound from when we'd lived close to a woods. The howl of an animal meeting a quick and violent death. My body shook. Cold sweat broke out all over me, as I pressed myself flat against the earth. Time passed, but I didn't hear anything but the waves. The sky was turning from black to gray. I had to get out of the field before it got light, before someone came out and saw me hiding there. My knees were shaking so hard I could barely make it up the road.

At home, I crawled into bed, staring at the ceiling. Something evil was going on in the black house. I remembered Dag's words. "One small girl is powerless to change destiny." I prayed for courage, and finally, I slept.

Sunday morning, I could hardly concentrate in church, and afterwards Aunt Julia insisted we drive to Pasadena. We toured the Huntington Library, where I tried to look interested in the historical documents. Afterwards, we went antiquing and picked out a couple of things for my room. Late in the afternoon, she suggested dinner at a French restaurant. I could tell she was trying to keep my mind off losing my necklace. She probably thought I was quiet because my sword was gone. That was partly true, but I was also trying to make sense of what I'd seen and heard last night. I told myself to think about something else. The answers would come.

Monday dawned clear and sunny with no wind, the kind of beach day they show in *Surfer Magazine*. I pulled on a leotard and my jungle-print baggies and ran downstairs. I was stretching my leg on the counter and finishing a banana muffin when a knock came on the back door. Greg waved at me through the frosted glass window, and I pulled the door open.

"Hi, kid." He wore a paint-spattered shirt and shorts, and his sun-streaked hair flopped over his forehead.

It felt good to see him. For a second, I could believe Rock Cove was a beach like any other beach, with surfers and volleyball players and swimmers having fun in the sun, instead of a place where shadowy figures met in the middle of the night to do unknown things. "You want a muffin?" I continued my exercise routine, lifting my foot onto the counter and flopping down over my leg.

"Doesn't that hurt?"

"Not any more. How about that muffin?"

"Nah. The Sunset Café serves hearty breakfasts." He stared at me. "Those are great-looking shorts."

"Thanks." I felt my cheeks grow hot.

"Come on. I've brought the stuff to do your room."

"Okay."

We walked out to the patio. "Hey, wait a minute." Greg stopped, hands on hips. "Show me something radical."

"What?"

"You know. Gymnastics."

I smiled. "Something radical, huh?"

"Rad and bad!"

I grinned. "I wasn't expecting a competition this morning, but I guess I could." I stretched my arms overhead, feeling loose and limber. "I'll show you part of my new floor routine. I'm going to use it to try out for the team when school starts. I call it *Above Storm Surf*."

"Hey, great."

"Here goes." One, two, three, four. I tapped my foot on the bricks, listening for the beat in my head. And then I lunged forward, into a handstand, over to a split position, double bent-leg position, up, over slowly. On my feet, body wave forward, body wave backward, then I was leaping through the air. One, two, three, four. Stag leap. Arch jump. The moves were flowing. My muscles had never felt this strong. Nothing could stop me now. I danced and turned and balanced and leaped. And lost all sense of time and place as I swooped like a giant bird over the ocean. Up on my toes, forward, down, up again. I finished with my final pose, body taut, arms in the air, head high. "Tah dah!" I bowed low, head touching my ankle.

"All right!" Greg whooped and clapped his hands.

"Thank you so much." I bowed again, wiping the sweat from my forehead.

"Kid, you're awesome." Greg opened the gate. "Olympic material, at least."

"Yeah, yeah. Tell me something," I said as we walked out the gate. "What color is your truck anyway? I don't think I've ever seen paint that bright."

He laughed and grabbed a ladder out of the back. "I call it Moonlight Green. I tried to get the color of the ocean when the plankton come in and the waves turn flourescent under the moonlight."

I shook my head. "Looks like lime juice under the sun to me."

"Hey, don't hurt my feelings, now."

"I'm not. I like it. Honest."

"It grows on you," he said.

I picked up a couple of cans of "Sweet Butter Yellow," the paint I'd chosen, and we strolled into the house and up the stairs. Classical music drifted from Aunt Julia's studio. She'd been working for hours already. The client from New York had her going crazy.

"Hey, Tory," Greg said. "How'd you like to learn to surf? Next month I won't be working as much, and I could teach you."

"That sounds fun." I'd always wanted to glide over the waves on a board. And it would be twice as fun with Greg as my teacher.

"Great. Let's do it then."

Upstairs, I helped Greg drape plastic over my bed and desk and bureau. He pried open a can, shoved a stick into the creamy liquid and stirred. Paint smell filled the air. "Lucky this room's been painted recently," he said. "No sanding necessary."

I gazed at the top of his head as he stirred. "Greg, did you notice my necklace is gone?"

He looked up. "No." He balanced the stick on top of the paint can and stared at me. "What happened? Did you lose it?"

"At the party."

"I'm sorry. I know how much that necklace meant to you."

"Yeah." I stared hard at the can of paint. I would not cry. "I just know it's in Dag's house."

"Did you ask him?"

"Aunt Julia called yesterday. He said it hasn't turned up." I looked quickly away.

"Geez. If I were working over there, I'd snoop around, but I won't be building his stage until he gets back from the tour."

"Wait a minute." I sat up straighter. "Didn't you tell me he goes sailing on Tuesdays?"

"Yeah."

"That's tomorrow. Does he always go at the same time?"

"Three o'clock. Why? What are you going to do?"

"I don't know. But I'll think of something."

He reached out, touched my hand. "Be careful, Tory, okay?"

"Why?" I sounded a little angry. "I thought Dag was such a great guy. Why are you telling me to be careful all of a sudden?"

Greg took a deep breath and let it out slowly. "I don't know. I just have a feeling you might be heading for trouble."

"Me too," I said. "But I don't have any choice."

116

CHAPTER

TWELVE

It was almost three o'clock, and I waited on our patio until I saw Dag's catamaran slice through the foam, heading for the open sea. His black hair streamed out behind him as the Hobie Cat bucked over the waves and caught the wind, racing south.

I took off running. On the point, the domed roof of Dag's house rose into the sky blocking out the sunlight. I stepped into the house's shadow, ready to ring the bell, but my finger halted in mid-air. *Wait a minute*! Elissa could get in big trouble for this. Why hadn't I thought of that before? She was probably forbidden to let anybody in the house. I stood there and stared at the door, my eyes burning. My sword was in there. It had to be. *Shoot!* I squeezed my hands together, turned around slowly and started walking away.

Loud knocking stopped me.

Elissa stood in the doorway. She waved her arms in the air, gesturing for me to come back. Should I go in? And then, before I could decide, she ran toward me, grabbed my arm and pulled me toward the house. She smiled at me, and I smiled back. She was surprisingly strong.

Inside the house, I looked quickly around. The immense wood floor shone with new wax, but no familiar gleam of gold met my stare. Across the room, a fire roared in the fireplace, lighting the the bull's teeth to fiery daggers.

There were so many questions I wanted to ask her. Why did you do that sketch of me with the sword? What about the girl in the bull's mouth? Why won't Dag let you talk to anybody? Have you seen my necklace? But if I came on too strong, she might pull back. I stayed quiet, letting her make the moves. She beckoned me to follow her, and we climbed the stairs.

I remembered the other night and how I'd

followed Dag down these stairs like a lovesick groupie. Like in a dream, things had happened, and there was nothing I could do to stop them. Now, I followed his daughter. But it was because I wanted to.

Shafts of light formed red bars on the hall carpet. Elissa turned to look at me, and her gray eyes urged me on. I padded down the hall after her, and we walked through an arched doorway. Light, white and gauzy as Elissa's blouse, filled this room, and I knew immediately it was hers. French doors stood open to let in the cool breeze and the sound of the waves. A high wooden bed with a white comforter took up most of one wall. Over it hung a painting of the rocks where Donna Jean had died.

How could she keep that picture over her bed? There was so much I didn't know about this strange girl. I wanted to ask her about the caped figures, but she probably didn't know about them.

Elissa moved to the balcony and gazed out the open glass doors. Her blouse billowed from her shoulders like wings. Her soft flower scent drifted to me as I stood next to her. "You love the ocean, don't you Elissa?"

She didn't move, just stared out to sea. A mile south, Dag's boat raced away through the water. He always stayed out at least an hour, Greg had told me, so we had some time.

"So do I." I touched her arm. "Did you know my mother died too? Maybe we can help each other to be less sad."

She turned large, tear-filled eyes on me, and I felt her hand tremble against mine. She led me across the room to a marble bureau, pulled a key from her pocket and unlocked the top drawer. She lifted out my tablet and handed it to me. I opened the cover, but the page was blank, and I slipped it into my back pocket.

Then she drew a photograph from the drawer. She brushed her fingertip over the photo and turned it slowly toward me. The picture was cracked, but its color was vivid and its lines sharp. On a stretch of sunny beach, a slender dark-haired woman held the hand of a smiling little girl. "Oh," I said. "You and your mother?"

She nodded.

"She's beautiful." I studied the tall, blue-eyed woman, and suddenly I drew in my breath in a sharp gasp. A tiny sword gleamed on the shoulder of her blouse.

I looked at Elissa.

She slipped the photo into the drawer, under a satin blouse, slightly yellowed with age. Two pin holes marred the yoke. She closed the door and locked it.

"Your mother wore a charm like mine. That's why you were so excited when we met."

She touched the hollow of her throat with her fingertip. Then she reached out and touched my throat. She formed a sword with her fingers.

"My necklace," I breathed. "Is it here?"

She tiptoed to the door, and checking the hallway, motioned me to follow her. At the end of the hall, she twisted the knob of a massive, arched door. She shoved the thick wood, and the door swung silently inward. A putrid smell swept into the hall.

Elissa tugged on my hand, and I followed her inside the high, curving room. Red light glowed in the dim atmosphere. Seconds went by as my eyes adjusted. The room must take up this whole part of the second story, I thought. To my left, the mountains rose through slits of tinted glass, and looking straight ahead, I saw the ocean through dim red windows. The pounding waves made only a soft whisper beyond the walls. Animal heads, mostly deer, stared out from wood paneled walls. Furs tumbled over the bed.

I stepped onto the red carpet, and my toe shoved into something cold and hard. I clapped a hand over my mouth. A bronze tub gaped below me. Inside was a lumpy, brownish-red mess. Once, during hunting season, I'd seen a neighbor clean a deer. Its insides had looked like that.

I pressed my hand over my nose, backing away.

Elissa pointed to a giant carved bureau. On top, a bronze urn in the shape of a bull's head leered down at us. Hundreds of drawers met my eyes, tiny ones on top, about two feet above us, growing larger and larger as they moved toward the bottom. I squeezed my fingers in and out. It would take forever to search them.

I walked over and yanked open a drawer in the middle. A pile of drawings lay inside. I stared at the sketch on top, feeling my heart shrivel inside me. In the picture, several caped figures stood around a fireplace filled with flames. Behind hoods, their faces were invisible except for two people. Dag and the person next to him. No! I screamed inside. No!

In the picture I wore a cape like the rest of the figures, and a long necklace. On the end of the chain, a bull's head glittered in the firelight. I slammed the drawer, turning to look at Elissa. Had she drawn this lie? "Why?" I asked.

She turned away and started opening drawers. She wasn't going to answer. Forget it, I told myself. You can ask her later. Quickly, I started pulling open drawers but found piles of clothes and other personal stuff. A leather jewelry box sat in the bottom drawer, and I held my breath as I opened it. But my necklace wasn't there among the watches and bracelets and cuff links. I looked around the room for a clock. There wasn't one. Why hadn't I bought that Swatch I'd seen in Beverly Hills? We opened, searched, and closed drawers, moving upward. And then all the drawers had been opened, and I still hadn't found my sword. On top, the urn shone in the late-afternoon light.

I moved across the room and grabbed a heavy wood chair. "Quick. Hold it steady for me, Elissa."

She grabbed the arms, and I hopped on top, reaching upward, but my groping fingers were at least two inches lower than the urn. I jumped down, looking quickly around the room, and ran to the bookshelf, grabbing several hefty volumes and stacking them on the chair. I climbed on top, perching on my toes as I reached up. My fingertips connected with cold metal.

The urn was heavy, and I almost lost my balance as I eased it over the edge and handed it down to Elissa. She looked inside, then back at me, and a smile lit up her face. I leaped down beside her, reached in and let out a sound of pure pleasure as I drew out my necklace. I squeezed it to my chest, breathing out a prayer of thanks.

"What are you girls doing?" The deep voice thundered through the doorway.

Elissa's hands flew into the air.

I let out a small cry and almost dropped the necklace. How could we have taken so long? How could we have forgotten?

Dag stepped into the room. His hair stuck out wildly from the wind, and his eyes glittered. When he spoke, his voice was low. "I don't remember inviting you here, Tory." He strode toward us. "And Elissa. You know better than to invade my privacy."

"It wasn't her fault," I said. "I wanted to look for my necklace. And I found it. Why did you tell Aunt Julia it wasn't here when you had it all the time?"

Dag's eyes drilled into me. "Elissa was a good girl until you came to Rock Cove, Tory."

"How can *you* talk about good? You *stole* my necklace," I hissed, too angry to care anymore.

Elissa shrank backward. Her mouth opened, and her eyes widened into two gray circles.

"Now, Lissy, it's all right," Dag said. "I know you didn't mean to be bad. You like Tory, don't you? You needn't worry. I'll take care of her." He held out a hand. The big ring glittered on his finger. "Come to me, Elissa."

Her features relaxed, and she walked slowly toward him. He took her hand and guided her toward the door. "That's my good girl. Go now. Finish the painting you began this morning." Without a backward a glance, she disappeared into the hallway.

He turned to me, and I felt my heart leap like an animal trapped in my chest.

The scar burned across his cheek. His eyes had a strange light in them. I could try to break for the door, but I knew my trembling legs could never carry me fast enough.

"So you found your sword." A slow smile spread across his face. Casually, he grabbed the urn and heaved it to the floor, where it tumbled over the carpet in soft thuds, finally clanging into the tub full of guts.

I took several steps backward. Dag moved quickly as a cat. Before I could even react, he'd swept my chain from my hand and into the air.

"Give me that!" I leaped into the air, fury driving me, and pounded on his chest and arms with my fists. It was like pounding on a boulder.

"It's mine. Give it to me!"

He stood there and let me pound, until my fists and arms ached with fatigue. Still, I didn't stop.

He laughed, soft and low.

With a moan, I let my arms drop to my sides. It was hopeless.

"Did you know Delia pulled this off you at the party and brought it to me?" He swung my necklace back and forth over his head. "She had such fun stealing from you. I suggested the black wig. She wants to be an actress, you know. I've repaired the chain and polished the gold. Your trinket is as good as new."

"Why would she do that?"

"For me, Tory. She would do anything for me. And you will too."

"I'll never do anything for you!"

He kneaded my sword through his fingers, staring at it. "Donna Jean wore a symbol like this. She flaunted it to hurt me." He snapped his head back. "Yes, to hurt me. She would not accept Elissa's heritage. The girl has the royal blood of the ancients in her veins, but Donna Jean wouldn't face the truth. She tried to interfere with Elissa's destiny. This little bauble kept my wife in rebellion. The sword of the spirit she called it. I had to get rid of it."

"You killed her, didn't you?"

"No. She killed herself."

"What are you going to do to Elissa?"

He smiled. "My daughter is not like other girls. She has been chosen to revive truth. In the new era, the world will be orderly. Sacrifice in exchange for power. And pleasure. There will be pleasure, Tory, unlike any you've ever known. Pure, sensual pleasure. Oneness with the universe." His words flowed through my head, mingling with the soft rush of the waves outside the windows. He raised his hand, rubbing his ring with his thumb. A sweet fragrance filled the air. The room softened, shimmered with pink light.

A memory floated into my mind. I was about five years old. Mom had a vase made out of cranberry glass, and I used to stare through it, into a blurry pink world. The fairy world, I called it and thought I'd always be happy if I could live in such a place.

"Join us, Tory. Be one with us."

The sweet smell bloomed in my head. Petals unfolding, filling my mind with pink light. "Come." Dag reached for my hand. "Let us see what the future holds."

Slowly, I raised my hand, let it slip into his. Dag's hand felt powerful around mine, and I knew he could lead me into worlds I could never enter on my own. We walked across the room. Below us, the bronze bucket gleamed. I looked down at it as if from a great height, smelling only sweetness.

Dag jerked his arm out, my chain dangling from his fingers. "Your heart and soul are here in my hand, Tory. They belong to Moloch now. Tell me you are Moloch's."

He lowered my sword toward the bucket of gore.

Light spun off the gold into my eyes. The room careened into red. The horrible odor stabbed into my senses. "No!" I lunged for my sword. "Give me that!"

He snatched it away, laughing. His other hand tightened like cold steel around my wrist.

"Let me go!" I tried to yank my arm away, but he pulled me toward him.

Panic exploded in my chest. I had to get away. Now! I glanced down. I bent at the knees, groped with my left hand, and jammed my fingers against cold metal. Curling my hand around the bucket's edge, I yanked with all my strength. Up and over. A sickening gush filled the air.

Dag's grip loosened. I jerked away. Dodging to my left, I sprinted around the smelly mess spreading over the carpet.

Dag's laughter followed me down the hall.

"You'll come back to me, Tory. We will worship together at the altar of Moloch."

"No I won't!" I screamed. But even as I yelled it, I wondered how I could fight him.

CHAPTER

THIRTEEN

I ran blindly up the road, lurching over bumps and nearly falling on my face a couple of times. Our house came into sight, and it looked better than I'd ever seen it.

"Hold it right there, kid." The familiar voice cut through my panic. Near our gate, Greg was loading tools into his truck. "Did you get your necklace?"

"No." I wiped furiously at the tears that spilled from my eyes.

"Wait a minute." Greg heaved a folding table into the truck bed and walked over to me. "Are you okay?" I felt his arm come around me. And, then I don't know what happened, but I lost it, really lost it. I cried long and hard into his shoulder. My arms closed around his hard torso. His T-shirt felt soft and warm against my blubbering face. "Dag has my necklace," I sobbed. "He's crazy."

Greg held my shoulders. "Calm down, now. No need to cry. I'll talk to him."

"No!" I yanked my head back to look at him. "Why not?"

"I'll get it back, don't worry." If Greg talked to Dag, he'd only deny everything. I couldn't stand it if Greg believed him over me. Like everybody else did.

He looked confused. "Okay, Tory." He wiped tears from my cheeks with his fingers. "If that's what you want."

"I, I d-d-do." My voice was wobbly, but the crying had stopped.

"I can't believe Dag would steal your necklace. He must have flipped out or something."

"No, he hasn't flipped out. He's always been crazy. It's just that he's suckered everybody around here into thinking he's some kind of hero."

"And me along with them?"

I nodded. "You, too."

Greg's brown eyes turned chocolate-soft. "I'd never be on Dag's side against you. Never."

"Well, thanks," I sniffled.

"I wish we could go for a burger and talk about it," he said. "But I'm driving into L.A. I need to finish a job first thing in the morning. Mom and Dad are coming back tomorrow night, and I want to spend some time with them."

"That's okay," I said.

"Don't do anything until I get back. Promise me." He reached out and smoothed a strand of hair off my my cheek. His fingertips were warm, slightly calloused. "We'll put our heads together and come up with a plan."

I pressed my hands to my sides.

"It's only one day, Tory. Try to be patient."

"Okay."

He held my hand as we walked around to the truck's door, but I was too upset to appreciate how good it felt.

He climbed inside and slammed the door. "Be careful, kid. I'll be back tomorrow night."

"Yeah." I gave him a small salute. "You, too."

Greg fired up the truck and drove away. A giant dust storm rose under the truck's bumping tires, as it careened up the road past Dag's house. The shiny yellow-green fenders glared in the sunlight. I almost screamed at him to stop and take me with him. In the city, we could eat junk food, go to a movie, maybe go dancing. Act like everything was normal. But it wasn't. And I wasn't going anywhere. I had questions. And there was one person who might have the answers.

Delia opened her door on my second knock, peering around the doorframe at me. I was all set to yell at her, but she looked like somebody had beat me to it. Her hair stuck up around her face, and her eyes were red. Mascara and eyeliner smudged her cheekbones. Her orange nails pressed against the white doorframe. "What do you want, Tory?"

"I want to talk to you."

"Well, I don't want to talk to you."

She started to push the door closed, but I darted in front of her into the hall. I was getting ruder and ruder all the time. "I want to ask you a question, Delia."

"Sshhh . . ." She glanced at a closed door across the living room. "Dad's in his study. I don't want to bother him."

"I'm not leaving until you talk to me."

"All right, then. Let's go to my room." She walked slowly down the hall, and I followed her inside a large room decorated in black and white. Cyclone posters covered the walls. An open suitcase filled with clothing sat on her striped comforter. She pointed to a round-backed chair by her empty desk. "Sit, if you want."

"I don't." I stared at her, hands on hips. "Is it true, Delia? Did you steal my sword?"

"I don't know what you're talking about."

"Dag told me you stole my necklace and gave it to him. True or false?"

She fiddled with a long, gold earring.

I took a step toward her. "Come on. Did you or didn't you steal my necklace?"

To my surprise, tears filled her eyes. "He said he'd get me a part in a movie. He promised." She flopped onto her bed. Tears rolled down her cheeks.

"And now he's blown you off?"

She nodded, rubbing at her face.

"What's he into? Was that you I saw the other night, wearing a cape, walking into the house? What went on that night, anyway?"

She looked up at me, and her skin was deathly-pale. "I don't know."

"You were there, after his party, weren't you?"

She pressed her lips together and looked away.

"What's the matter? Did Dag threaten you?"

She lifted her hands, then let them drop into her lap. "Don't ask me. Please."

"I'm not going to stop until you tell me the truth about Dag."

"I can't," she whispered.

"Delia . . ." Dr. K's voice came from outside the door. "Are you ready, dear? Our cab will be here in five minutes."

"Yes, Dad. I'm packed."

I felt a burning sensation in my stomach. "Where are you going?"

"To my mom's. For the rest of the summer."

"I don't believe you."

She shrugged. "You heard my Dad. The cab

136

will be here in five minutes. He's flying up with me." She let out a laugh. "I guess he doesn't trust me to get on the plane myself. He thinks I'm obsessed with Dag. He wants to get me away from him."

"But Dag's leaving on tour the day after tomorrow."

"Guess Dad's afraid I'll run away with him or something."

"Would you?"

She shrugged, and her eyes reminded me of the shiny, trapped eyes of Dag's deer trophies on his wall. "I don't know. I might. If he asked me to. I do anything he tells me. Sometimes, I don't want to, but I do it anyway. I don't know why. He's just so . . . so . . ."

"Powerful?" I asked.

"Yes." She looked out the window where yellow hibiscus blooms brushed against the glass. "At first it wasn't like that. I just thought he was awesome-looking, and he'd done a few rock videos, and I was impressed. His music was incredible. And he said he'd help me with my acting. Then, it got so I couldn't stand to be away from him. I guess I love him."

She'd taken my necklace for him. I didn't even need to ask her again. I remembered how I felt when he was close to me and I smelled his sweetness and looked into his silver-blue eyes. Cold sweat broke out on my forehead. Would I do anything for him, too? I shoved my hands in my pockets. "I don't think you love him, Delia. Not really. He can do that to people. Suck them in. Make them like him more than they should."

She shrugged.

"Maybe it was your dad's idea for you to leave Rock Cove for awhile, but you're not fighting him on it. So you're making your own choice in that way."

Red veins ran through the whites of her eyes. "Do you feel sucked in by Dag?"

"Sometimes. But I like Elissa more. And I think she's in trouble."

Delia nodded.

"What is it Delia? What's he going to do to her?"

"I don't know."

Outside, a horn honked.

I squeezed my hands into fists. I wanted to scream at her to give me answers. But I knew it wouldn't do any good. She was a lot more scared of Dag than she was of me.

"The truth is, I don't know anything about Elissa. I only know Dag's planning a special ceremony. Tomorrow night. And I'm not invited."

"But you don't know what this 'ceremony' is going to be?"

"No." She slammed her suitcase closed and clicked the locks. "He won't tell me." She looked up at me, and the sadness in her eyes made me catch my breath. "I've done some bad things, Tory. I only hope God will forgive me."

I swallowed hard. "What? What have you done?"

She shook her head violently, grabbed her suitcase and ran to the door. "Dad," she called. "I'm ready. Let's go."

I grabbed her arm. "Tell me."

"Let go of me!" She pulled away. "If you knew what was good for you, you'd leave too. Go back home to Massachusetts. Stay with your friends. Just get out of here."

"Why?"

Dr. K. walked through the doorway of his

study, carrying an overnight bag. He looked surprised to see me. "Why, Tory. How nice of you to drop by to see Delia off." For a minute, I felt guilty. Maybe if I'd visited her earlier . . . but I couldn't worry about that now.

"Tory's just going, Dad. Come on." Delia rushed through the door. "We don't want to miss our plane."

"Of course. Tell Julia I'll be home Friday." Dr. K. smiled at me.

"I will." I walked through the doorway.

Delia slammed the cab door and stared straight ahead as Dr. K. locked the house. Seconds later, the cab bumped past me, with Delia still sitting like a statue, and Dr. K. giving me a wave.

At home, I ran upstairs to my room and closed the door. Fading sunlight washed the walls in a dim yellow light. Soon it would be night. A lonely feeling came down over me, as dark as the night about to descend on Rock Cove.

You will come back to me. Dag's words echoed in my head. *You will worship with me at the altar of Moloch.*

No! I told myself. I'll never do that! But I felt like David aiming his tiny slingshot at Goliath. Except that my slingshot was gone. Now, I had to fight him with my bare hands, and I'd seen how far that got me. Physically, I was no match for Dag and never would be, even if I had the little sword at my neck to give me courage.

I sat on my bed and felt something hard in my back pocket. The tablet. I pulled it out and leafed through the pages. Something was written on a page toward the back. The pencil marks were light, and when I was finally able to read the letters, they didn't make sense. The message was a question. A question I couldn't understand much less answer. "Is the bull my destiny?" I sank onto my bed. I *don't know, Elissa.* I *wish* I *could help you, but* I *just don't know how.*

Dinner that night was strained and silent. I could barely choke down my food. Should I tell Aunt Julia about my sword and the note from Elissa? I sighed inwardly. What evidence did I have? My aunt, like everyone else around here, was totally snowed by Dag's phony do-gooder attitude.

We'd just started clearing the table, when

the telephone rang. I carried the dishes to the sink, rinsed them and slipped them into the dishwasher. When I'd put the last glass in the rack, Aunt Julia was still on the phone. Her voice was low, business-like.

I climbed the stairs to my bedroom. Even though the room was huge, everything looked warm and cozy. Yellow paint and flowered wallpaper had transformed the grayness into a light, airy place. This room had the same cheerful feeling as my old one but was more sophisticated than that long-ago little-girl room on the Cape.

I switched on the lamp on my bureau, and soft peach-colored light shone through the shade. It made me feel good to know that Greg was part of it, that his hands had made it into a place I could love. Maybe I'd been silly to tell him not to talk to Dag. But Dag had all the answers. I wasn't ready to trust anybody, not even Greg, with my fight.

I slid a cassette into the player, turned up the volume and forced my mind into total concentration as I moved through the steps of *Above Storm Surf*. I pushed hard, showing my limbs no mercy, and my muscles responded until the turns, balances and poses blended together in one fluid motion. No question, I would make the team at my new school. I had never performed better in my life. I gave myself to the music and the strong feeling that came from mastering the intricate moves.

Two hours later, I switched off the machine. Drenched with perspiration, I stood in a cool shower. Once in my sleepshirt, I walked to the top of the stairs. Aunt Julia's voice rose from the living room. "Go ahead, Lonnie. Give me the figures so I can call the contractor." I climbed into bed.

Outside my window, the waves rushed in, sucking against the sand. I thought of the sketch I'd found and my face peering out at me from among the caped figures. I thought of Dag waving my necklace over his head, taunting me. It was a war between us now. Maybe it always had been. Stop, I told myself. Think of something else. Delia had told me to get away, go back to Massachusetts. I couldn't get on a plane, but I could go there in my mind.

I turned my face to the window. Stars

glittered in the sky like white Christmas lights. Silent night. Holy night. Christmas seemed so far away. Like it would never come again. I hummed the familiar carol and let my mind drift back to happy times.

I loved Christmas more than any time of year. Every Christmas Eve, Mom and I roasted a turkey with all the trimmings. Dad always insisted on making his geeky apple pie that collapsed when he took it out of the oven. "Tastes yummy in the tummy, honey. That's all that counts." He said the same thing every year. We smothered the mushy pie with vanilla ice cream, and it tasted a lot better than it looked. My mouth watered thinking about it. Later, the three of us opened our gifts by the fireplace, and we always left a little pie for Santa.

On Christmas morning, Dad read the story of the birth of Jesus from Luke, and we'd open our stockings. Afterward, Mom put out bowls of oyster stew on the Christmas-holly tablecloth. My nose wrinkled remembering the fishy taste. Yuk! The dish was a family tradition that went all the way back to the Pilgrims, according to Mom, and she couldn't stop doing it because all our ancestors up in heaven were watching. I hated the stuff, but I'd give up my new room for a bowl of Mom's oyster stew right now. If I'd only known then how precious those times were and what a comfort they could be to me when I felt myself, as now, in a storm of terrible darkness.

I slid out of bed and walked to the bureau. I reached into my cluster of shells and pulled out the picture of Mom and me under the Christmas tree.

Slipping back under my quilt, I studied the picture. Aunt Julia was right. I looked like Mom. I touched the beloved face under the cold glass, pictured her sitting on the bed next to me, like she used to after I'd been out with friends. We'd talk, and she'd tuck me in and kiss my forehead. I pressed the picture to my chest. Part of her would always live inside me.

Elissa missed her mom as much as I missed mine. Her love for Donna Jean was one of the things that drew us together, and now that I'd seen her mother's picture, I realized she lived in Elissa like Mom lived in me. And somehow we were all connected, because her mother had worn a sword like mine.

I squeezed my eyes closed, remembering how terrified Elissa looked when Dag caught us in his room. Was she moving closer to some horrible fate? Did it have anything to do with the ceremony planned for tomorrow night?

I had to do something to help her!

But what?

146

CHAPTER

FOURTEEN

A note was propped on the breakfast bar the next morning when I came downstairs. My aunt had gone into the city and wouldn't be back until dinner. Grabbing a bran muffin, I headed for the beach. The ocean's cool, hissing foam splashed around my legs as I marched along the shore toward the black tower. A searing breeze blew my hair around my shoulders. Unseasonal desert winds, Aunt Julia called the gusts that whipped up from the canyons.

The sun dazzled white against the sand, but a thin sheet of ice seemed to slide over my skin as I stepped into the shadow. Elissa's balcony was empty. Part of me was glad. I stared up at the black house, wondering what I'd say to her if she came out and looked down at me with her pleading eyes.

The roar of the waves and whir of the wind faded to an eerie hush. Hugging my arms to my sides, I remembered the first day I'd seen this place and how it reminded me of Dad's book on ancient temples. If only Dad were here now. I reached for my necklace, and a rush of sadness went through me as I touched bare skin. *Dad, I miss you so much.*

Tears stung my eyes. Around me, the air was still. I was all alone. Or was I? I thought about Dad and all the times we'd worked together on projects. All the times he'd called me Ms. Logic.

You need to fight, Tory!

Dad? I held very still, listening.

Use your talents to fight.

My talents. I thought for a minute. Gymnastics? What other talents did I have?

Logic!

Ms. Logic knows there's an answer for everything. But where? Where do I find the answers?

I stood, waiting, listening, and a memory

flashed into my mind. Last February, I'd had to do a history report on the Industrial Revolution. I hated that subject more than anything we'd learned all year. For days, I'd gone around the house grumbling, "I can't do this stupid thing."

Finally, Dad got exasperated with me. "Just plunge in, sweetheart. Go into my library, pull down a couple of texts and start reading. The answers will come." In desperation, I'd taken his advice. The answers were there. I got a B on the report.

The answers were there! There! The sand burned into the soles of my feet as I ran over the beach. I crossed the patio, raced up the stairs and threw open my closet. The carton of books felt like a box of lead as I slid it toward my bed. Plopping down on my carpet, I looked inside.

On top, a heavy text lay at an angle. *The Sacred and the Profane: The Nature of Religion.* I pulled it out, paged through the dusty smelling pages. It was so big, so thick. How could I find what I was looking for? I didn't even know what I was looking for. Not really. Something about rites. I turned to the index. Nothing. Tossing it aside, I pulled out a big blue book and scanned it, shaking my head as I tried to make sense of words like *immolation* and *cosmogony*. I tried another, and another.

Morning turned to afternoon as I paged through volume after volume, and came up empty. I reached for the next-to-last book, a thin red volume. *Ancient Pagan Cults*. I opened it to the Introduction.

Out tumbled a valentine card. One of those dumb little things you buy in boxes of a hundred or so. On the front, a muscle man lifted a barbell over his head. "Dad, you're strong, you're courageous, you're champion of my heart." I'd signed my name in thick red letters with "Love" written above it. I pressed the card in my fingers. My eyes moved back to the book. "Excellent analysis," Dad had written in his wide script. This is the one, I thought. The one with the answers.

"Lately, there has been a resurgence of interest in pagan cults and the black arts," the introduction read. I turned to the table of contents. Chapter Six was titled "The Phoenicians." I turned there and read.

"Scholars conjecture that the Phoenicians, with their expert knowledge of the sea, actually sailed to America two and a half millennia before Columbus. It is believed these seamen landed in the New World and settled in the area that became eastern Tennessee, where their descendents live to this day."

I lowered the book to my lap. It was true. Dag's people had come to America centuries ago. And Elissa was going to Tennessee tomorrow. Fear tingled through me. What would happen to her there?

Scanning the next few pages, I read that the ancients predicted the future by reading signs in animal intestines, that priests slashed their faces to appease the gods, that fire was worshipped and feared. It all fit—even Dag's scar. Among the priests' occultic talents was the power to cast spells, using amulets such as rings. I thought of the honey-sweet smell and the trance-like state I'd felt with it. Could Dag do those things?

"Ritual Practices" headed the next section. I read the subtitle underneath: "Human Sacrifice: A Major Part of Phoenician Religious Ritual." Human sacrifice? No way!

"Tory, darling."

My head snapped up.

Aunt Julia stood in the doorway. "I knocked but you didn't answer. Are you all right?"

"Yes." I tossed the book aside and jumped to my feet.

Aunt Julia looked elegant in her business suit, her light brown hair smooth against her cheek. "Darling, I'm sorry I had to abandon you this morning, and last night I was on the phone until all hours. There's been another emergency with my New York client. He wants a dinner meeting this evening at his hotel in Los Angeles, and I'm afraid it's a command performance. The project lives or dies on my being there tonight." She checked her gold watch. "I'm running late. There is chicken salad in the refrigerator, and there are peaches and bananas and . . ."

"You didn't have to come all the way home to tell me that, Aunt Julia. You could have called."

"I know, darling, but I felt dreadful leaving you this morning, and then being away all evening too."

"I'll be fine, Aunt Julia."

She smiled. "I know you will, dear. And as soon as I'm done with this project, we'll spend more time together. How does a trip to Santa Barbara sound? Now, don't forget the Howatts will be home later this evening if you need anything. I might be late." She held out her arms, and I walked into them, hugging her longer and harder than usual.

"See you in the morning, darling." She squeezed my shoulders and kissed me on the cheek. Then she was gone. A few minutes later, I heard her Mercedes purr up the road.

Flopping down by the bed, I picked up the red book and turned to the page I'd lost when Aunt Julia interrupted me. I swallowed hard as I read about a horror I didn't even want to contemplate. "Children and adults were burned to death in sacrificial rites to the god, Moloch. These burnings are evidenced by charred human and animal bones excavated in the neighborhoods of Phoenician altars. Thousands of urns filled with scorched bones of children have been recovered in Carthage."

Sickness churned in my stomach, and I

squeezed my eyes closed until the nausea passed. I didn't want to read more, but I had to know all of it. I focused on the page. "To offer a living human being was the highest form of sacrifice and performed when something crucial was desired, such as a victory in battle. Moloch, insatiable devourer of human victims, is often represented by a bull's head."

I read until the room turned dark and the ink blurred in front of my eyes. Was Dag planning that kind of horrible death for Elissa? What could he want so much that he'd trade his own daughter for it? I threw the book down and stared at the dark windows. My mind worked back over everything that had happened since the Fourth of July, trying to pull it all together.

Kelsey was out of the group. Cyclone was going on tour with Dag as the lead singer. This was his chance for real fame. With the power of celebrity, he could preach his religion all over the world. And he didn't believe in death, not like I did. The first time we'd met, he'd told me death was just a journey to another life. But I knew death was nothing to seek, nothing to inflict.

I leaned back against my bed. Fire. To be

burned alive in a fire. I wrapped my arms around my knees. The choking smoke. The searing flames. The firemen had reassured me that Mom and Dad died before the flames got to them. But Moloch's victims were forced alive into the fire. Could Dag really be planning that kind of torture for Elissa?

Wind slammed against the bedroom windows. I reached out, opening the front cover of the book with my index finger. Just looking at Dad's handwriting made me feel better. There was something in the left corner of the cover. Small writing I hadn't seen earlier. *Take up the sword of the Spirit*. Yes, I thought. My necklace was gone, but I had a weapon no one could take away from me. The power inside me to fight back.

I walked downstairs to the kitchen and opened the refrigerator. The thought of food made me sick, but I knew I had to eat. I crunched on an apple and forced several bites of chicken salad down my tight throat.

Outside, the waves pounded out a heavy beat. I crossed the living room and stared out at the rising moon. The ocean stretched darkly away, connecting with the sky in a black line at the horizon. Greg's house was dark. No one home yet.

I turned and walked slowly upstairs. Opening my bureau drawer, I took out my gymnastics gear, slipping into tights and a leotard. I snapped on gymnastics slippers, shoved my hands into guards, and pulled on a navy blue sweatshirt, smoothing my hair underneath the hood. In the mirror, my pale, freckled face stared back at me.

My hand moved to my throat, but no familiar feel of gold met my touch. I took a deep breath and headed downstairs, knowing something that turned my blood to ice.

If Dag caught me, he would kill me.

CHAPTER

FIFTEEN

I pushed the back door open and stepped into the night. I passed the Howatts' house, and as the ground curved uphill toward the point, I crossed the road and ran into the field bordering the cliff.

A gust of wind flattened the weeds around me. Headlights shot around the corner. I dropped to the ground, squeezing my eyes closed against the sudden glare. Ice plant squished against my cheek, and my pounding heart swelled to drown out the crickets. Musky earth smells seeped into my nostrils. I waited. No one came.

On my feet again, I crept up the road to the

point, slipping around the side of Dag's house. A red glow came from the second story windows. The smell of chimney smoke tinged the air. Beyond the point, the moon lit a path over the water. Below me, waves hissed and roared like a pack of hungry lions.

My stomach knotted as I studied the surface of the house. Stones jutted out to form uneven ledges with long stretches between them. A faint light shone from Elissa's bedroom. *Please be there, Elissa. I'm coming for you.*

The wall of the house appeared even more sinister in the faint moonlight. Its stones formed dark faces. Their misshapen mouths seemed to threaten me, whispering warnings into the night.

Slowly, purposefully, I climbed, forcing myself to breathe evenly, as if I were in competition. I imagined myself a giant spider, arms and legs spread to balance on the ledges. My feet, clad in the soft slippers, curled around the rocks. My hands, protected by the guards, grabbed slices of stone. Two steps. Three. The wall felt clammy under my fingers.

Above me, Elissa's balcony loomed. Below,

the sea swirled over deadly rocks. *Don't look down!* Wind gusted around the house. I flattened myself against the wall, grasping the ledges with both hands. A rock scraped my cheek. My right foot slipped against something sharp. Pain shot through my heel into my calf. The slab crumbled under me, and my foot kicked into empty air. Pieces of stone pinged down, down into the surf. Waves of fear broke inside me. The rocks below waited to shatter me like they had Donna Jean.

Mom! Dad! My fists closed tighter around my shaky handholds. The wind and waves pounded in my head. My fingers trembled, grew weak. I was going to fall. Dag would keep Elissa for Moloch, and no one would ever know. My courage crumbled and fell like the stones.

Nothing can harm you in love's circle, Tory.

Mom! The beloved voice bubbled up inside me.

"Oh, Mom, my sword is gone . . ." A sob escaped my throat.

But love surrounds you. The voice came from deep within me. I took deep breaths, fighting for calm. Pressing my forehead against stone, I prayed for strength. Gentle arms seemed to enfold me, hold me steady. Slowly, my body quieted. The trembling stopped.

My muscles felt strong again. I ran my foot along the wall, touched a smooth surface. A ledge. I'm going to make it, I told myself. A current of energy ran through my body. I steadied myself, climbing surely as if powerful hands pulled me up. Quickly, easily, one foot after the other.

At the balcony, I grabbed the cold concrete and hoisted myself onto the deck. I crouched there, under the wind, getting my bearings. The glass doors rattled in a violent gust. Behind them a faint orange glow lit Elissa's room. My heart fell. The room was empty.

I crept across the balcony. The doors gave way under my shove. I crossed the room, and in the hallway, a harsh crackling sound met my ears. The smell of smoke pricked at my throat. I tiptoed to the rail, and crouching down, looked into the room below.

A trickle of perspiration slid down my back. My cheek was warm and sticky with blood where I'd scraped it. I wiped my forehead on my sleeve.

Below me, flames rioted in the giant fireplace, hissing and crackling. Their light bathed the masks and statues in a blood-red glow. Scattered around the room, tall candelabras held flickering candles. Fire roared from the jaws of the bull, bursting out to lick the air with orange tongues.

Dag, wearing something red and flowing, stood behind Elissa, his hands on her shoulders. They stared into the flames. Elissa's white gown billowed from her neck to her bare feet, her braided hair coiling in a satin rope down her back.

Dag turned suddenly, and his cape shimmered like red water in the firelight. He looked up.

Cold perspiration broke out on my forehead.

"Tory!" His long black hair caught the light. "You're there, aren't you? Look, Elissa. She's come to join us." He turned her, gently tilted her chin up. She looked up, searching for me.

I rose and stepped out of the shadows.

He laughed, and the sound turned my heart to blowing sand. "Moloch is pleased with your courage, Tory. You are stronger than I realized. Come." He lifted an arm, and the ring flashed in the firelight as he moved to the stairs. "Join us."

Slowly, I backed away from the banister. Soft music, like water tumbling over rocks, drifted up from below.

Elissa stared at me as I walked down the stairs, her eyes huge in her pale face. The familiar honey-like scent poured over me, and the air glowed with pink light. I tried to shake away the warm, liquid feeling inside. Tried to remember why I'd come. But the evil in Dad's book faded from my mind like a long-forgotten horror movie.

At the bottom of the stairs, Dag met me. His fingers moved to my neck, and I felt their tips, smooth and cool against my throat. He pulled a thick chain from his cape and slipped it over my head. He untied my hood, slid it down over my hair. "That's better. A woman's hair is her glory." His eyes moved over my face, and in them I saw a world of pleasure—a world I could only imagine. The thought of experiencing all the mysteries with him brought waves of excitement inside me. I looked down at the bull's head lying against my chest, shining like a giant ruby.

"You will wear amethyst combs when you become my priestess." His eyes flashed from silver to deep blue. "That is what you want, isn't it Tory? To be mine, to come with me on tour, to have the world at your feet?"

"Yes," I said.

Taking my hand, he led me toward Elissa. I stared into her eyes. He lifted her hand, gave it to me. Her fingers lay limp and cold in mine. "Do you want to be her sister?" Dag asked.

"Yes," I told him.

He rested a hand on my shoulder. "Your decision will not be cheap. On the contrary, commitment is expensive. Molk is required. Do you understand?"

"No." I stared at Elissa.

"Molk. Sacrifice." Dag walked to the fireplace and pushed a hand against the wall next to it. A narrow door swung open. He thrust his arms inside and drew out a bronze slab. He released legs from underneath and rolled the table silently toward us. Outside, the sea raised its voice in mournful cries against the rocks.

"The topheth," Dag said as he moved the table to the edge of the flames. "It is time to prepare for the sacrifice."

"Where are the others?" I asked.

He looked at me. "The others?"

"The ones that were here before. . ."

Something like a growl came from his throat. "They were not worthy, Tory. This is your spiritual awakening. I am your mentor. No one else may share this time with us."

Dag raised both hands toward the bull. "Give me your power, Moloch. The world will worship you, and you alone."

He reached into his cape, took out a wisp of black satin and moved to Elissa. He drew her hands together in front of her and tied the cloth around her wrists. She looked down at the floor, not fighting him. "You know I cannot grieve, Elissa. I must give you up gladly to gain the power."

He scooped her up in his arms and laid her gently on the bronze table. Her gray eyes stared into mine. She looked so beautiful, so peaceful, lying there, as if she were sunbathing on a sunny afternoon. But her eyes seemed to cry out to me. *What is it, Elissa? What do you want to tell me?* I walked toward her.

He drew out another scrap of black and slipped it over her head. "Don't be afraid, Elissa." His words flowed into the room like cool water. "Moloch will guide you into your next life. We will meet again." He rolled the table toward the flames. Fire drooled from the bull's jaws. A spark sizzled on Elissa's dress.

"Wait!" I grabbed the edge of the table. "I need to see her eyes."

He smiled at me. "Of course, Tory. One last goodbye is permitted." He slipped the hood up over her face.

I stared hard into Elissa's eyes. Why was she looking at me like that? What had I come here for? Was it to say goodbye? Her pupils reflected the gold of the raging fire. Shining gold, reminding me of something . . .

Dag slipped the hood over her face, grabbed the edge of the table and pushed.

The sword!

"No!" I screamed. "Stop!" I grabbed the table and pulled it toward me, slapping furiously at the sizzling places on her dress. I ripped the hood off her head. "You are not Moloch's!" I screamed. "You're not!"

She slipped off the table.

I gave her a small shove. "Run, Elissa!"

She lunged for the stairs.

"Come here, girl." Dag sprang at her like a panther. One arm lashed out, grabbed her braid. She stumbled backward, and a whimper of pain came from her lips. The first sound I'd ever heard from her lips.

"Let her go!" I vaulted onto his back, burying my fingers in his long black hair. I yanked the thick strands as hard as I could.

He staggered. Elissa pulled free.

"Run, Elissa." I pounded with my fists, felt my hands batter hard muscle.

Elissa raced up the stairs, her white dress billowing out behind her.

Dag jerked upright, throwing me to the floor. Pain tore through my hip. He ripped off his cape. A candelabra crashed to the floor. "Heretic!" He raised his fist.

I scrambled behind a couch as the tapestries exploded into flames. The fire leaped across the room as if forced by an invisible wind. Flames attacked the wood paneling, the sofas, the stairway. Smoke surged into the air. The fumes burned my eyes. My lungs screamed for air.

Grabbing a stone horse off a pedestal, Dag leaped on the stairs. He heaved the statue onto the bottom steps, crashing them to splinters. He bounded upstairs toward Elissa.

"Run, Elissa!" I ripped the ugly bull from my neck and threw it into the flames. A wave of heat slammed over me. My head jerked up as a mad, evil roar filled the room, thundering against the walls. The bull's teeth flashed orange in the fire. Was I going to die here? I threw my hands into the air. My fingers collided with something rough. A pillar. Flames licked at the white column.

I had to vault or be burned alive.

CHAPTER

SIXTEEN

Crouching, I willed all my strength into my knees and legs, ignoring my throbbing hip. I let go. My body slammed into hot stone. Flames seared my heels as I shinnied upward, the fire roaring below me. I reached the second story ledge and pulled myself into the hallway.

Dag strode down the hall toward Elissa. "Moloch will have you! And *you*!" He turned to jab an arm in my direction.

Elissa swayed unsteadily in the black smoke. Her hands writhed, and she ripped the bindings from her wrists. Dag lurched toward her. "It is your destiny." He grabbed her arm.

The stairway collapsed with a thundering

crash.

Flames exploded through the hallway, and I smelled the thick remembered scent of burning carpet. The rail burst into flame. I dropped to the floor, crawled under the smoke toward Dag, breathing air that stabbed my lungs like hot knives.

A shriek pealed through the hallway. "Murderer!" I looked up. Elissa was screaming! "Mama wouldn't go in the fire. You chased her. You pushed her. Mama . . . Mama . . . The rocks . . ." Her voice, silent so long, screamed accusations.

"Quiet, daughter!" Dag bellowed. He forced her arms to her sides. "Your mother betrayed me. She would not embrace her destiny, but you will."

"Leave her alone!" I hurtled along the floor toward them.

"No!" Elissa wrenched her arms from his grip. "I will never go to Moloch! Never!" Her voice rang out strong and clear over the roar of the fire. "I am Mama's. I belong to her God."

I ran to stand beside Elissa.

"Moloch needs flesh . . . " Dag let out a

gagging sound as if an unseen hand had grabbed him by the throat. He stumbled backward into the burning railing. His arms flew out, and his shining eyes bulged in their sockets. Zig-zags of flame leaped over the railing to clutch at him. Fire flashed up the sleeves of his shirt. The sharp smell of burning hair filled the air. I took a step toward him, but the rail broke in a sickening crunch. With a long howl, he disappeared into the holocaust below.

A thunderous explosion came then, bursting the bull's head. Fiery shards soared around us, crashing against the walls. Elissa fell against me.

I coughed painfully. We had to get air! I dragged her down the burning hall through Dag's room to the doors facing the mountains. The locked knob was hot in my fingers. Frantically, I looked around. The bull's head urn lay on the floor. Empty. I heaved it into the glass. Yanking off my sweatshirt, I swept the glass aside and dragged Elissa onto the balcony. I fell to my knees on the stone ledge, exhausted, gulping in great breaths of air. Smoke poured from the room. Somewhere, sirens shrieked.

Tears spilled down Elissa's cheeks. "He killed her," she cried. "He killed Mama."

I patted her thin back. "I know. I'm sorry, Elissa. So sorry. But he can't hurt us now."

A bolt of flame shot from the nearby balcony. "We have to get out of here."

"I know." Elissa struggled to breathe. Her head fell forward. She collapsed next to me.

I tried to get up but felt as if I were moving through boiling water. Crawling on my belly, I pushed forward, dragging us both to the edge of the balcony. Air. *We need air.* But the flames sucked away all oxygen. Any minute, I would pass out too. I hung over the balcony. And then, I saw it. A glint of green metal. "Greg," I screamed. "We're here! Up here!"

"Tory?" a yell came. "What the . . .?"

"Your ladder," I yelled.

"Hold tight!"

I fought for oxygen as Greg raised the ladder in what seemed to be slow motion. He stepped onto the bottom rung and began to climb. His hair whipped back from his forehead in the firestorm as sparks sizzled around him. He grasped the ladder, pulling himself up. His head was tipped back, and his brown eyes shone with fiery light.

"Hurry," I breathed. "Please, Greg. Hurry."

Then, he was on the balcony, grabbing my hand, pulling me to my feet. "Tory!" he yelled. "Are you okay?"

"Yes, but Elissa . . ."

"I've got her." He reached down and lifted her into his arms, heaving her over one shoulder.

"Go, Tory!" he yelled.

I stuck a tentative foot over the edge of the ladder, steadying myself on the thick rung. Down, down, down, I climbed until blessed ground touched the soles of my feet. Greg and Elissa followed above me. The minute my feet touched the earth, I ran. Away from the fire. Away from the horror.

We stopped at the edge of the cliff. Greg let Elissa's feet slide to the ground, holding her around the waist with his arm.

Her eyes opened, and she coughed. She took a few deep breaths. Her paleness turned to a blush I'd never seen before, and her gray eyes seemed to glow with health.

I touched her arm. "Are you okay?"

She looked up at the black house. "It's burning." A slow smile curved her lips.

"You're talking!" Greg said.

"Yes," she said. "I am fine."

"Good girl." Greg patted her shoulder, then turned to me. "What about Dag?"

"He's in there," I said. "It's almost like the fire . . . wanted him."

A hook and ladder screamed around the corner. Gusts of wind whipped the flames above us to a frenzy, showering the field with sparks. "Wait here," Greg said. "I'll talk to the firemen." He sprinted off.

Elissa smiled up at the black house, then turned to me. "The bull is gone. And we're alive."

"I know, Elissa. We won the war."

She stared into my eyes, then reached to her collar and unbuttoned the white lace fabric. When I saw what was there, a sweet joy leaped up inside me. My sword gleamed at her throat.

She unclasped my chain and fastened the sword around my neck. "Sisters." She held out her arms.

We hugged each other. Dag had talked about destiny, but he hadn't seen what we'd sensed all along. Elissa's and my destiny was the same.

"Sisters," I said.